RULERS AND SUBMISSIVES OF
SUBJUGATION

RULERS AND SUBMISSIVES OF
SUBJUGATION

CHRISTOPHER TREVOR

 iUniverse®

RULERS AND SUBMISSIVES OF SUBJUGATION

iUniverse books may be ordered through booksellers or by contacting:

iUniverse
1663 Liberty Drive
Bloomington, IN 47403
www.iuniverse.com
1-800-Authors (1-800-288-4677)

Because of the dynamic nature of the Internet, any web addresses or links contained in this book may have changed since publication and may no longer be valid. The views expressed in this work are solely those of the author and do not necessarily reflect the views of the publisher, and the publisher hereby disclaims any responsibility for them.

Any people depicted in stock imagery provided by Thinkstock are models, and such images are being used for illustrative purposes only.
Certain stock imagery © Thinkstock.

ISBN: 978-1-4917-8569-0 (sc)
ISBN: 978-1-4917-8570-6 (e)

Library of Congress Control Number: 2015920917

Print information available on the last page.

iUniverse rev. date: 12/29/2015

TITLE: PORN RING BUST GONE BUST
Author: Christopher Trevor

Story Inspired by: series of pics entitled "Self Strip" as featured on the hotter than hot website "BootLust.com"

Story dedicated to my internet buddy: Justin Tyler- Ormond and to handsome tall-booted cops everywhere.

I had been following the case known as "Porn to Scorn" for the last two months, although my sergeant, the detective involved in the case and other superiors at the precinct didn't know that. I suppose it can be said that when the time came to finally break up the illegal porn ring I wanted to be the hero cop that did it. And once I blew the lid on the porn ring I saw a huge promotion to detective for me in the works. I would go from being Police Officer Jody Harman to Detective Harman overnight.

We knew that the camera store called "Rollies" on Avenue A. and West Seventh Street in New York City was actually a front for a group who called themselves "Porn to Scorn", but their name was only known in certain circles. The way this group created porn movies was through blackmail. The actors that they used in their films had all reported that they had been somehow blackmailed or coerced into performing for the rogue filmmakers. One young high-powered junior executive who works for a top of the line prestigious company in the Wall Street area told of how he had received a DVD in the mail at his workplace, anonymously.

The note enclosed with the DVD said to watch the film privately. So, after everyone in the office had left for the day the junior executive (who will have to remain nameless for the obvious reasons) slid the DVD into the player in his computer and nearly fell off his chair when he saw what was on it. It was him...and a drop-dead sexy prostitute who called herself "Candy" that the junior executive had taken back to his hotel room while on a recent business trip. He sat there at his desk, aghast, grunting and coughing uncontrollably as he was not able to breathe properly...watching himself fuck the tar out of the beautiful high-priced prostitute.

Midway through the DVD the junior executive heard a voiceover saying that if he did not do as he was told when further instructions came...*and they would*...the next copy of the DVD would be sent to his wife at her workplace...and if he still refused to do as the instructions he would receive dictated, then the next copy would go to his superiors in the company he worked for. As the junior executive sat there sweating and tugging beyond nervously at his hundred dollar silk tie the voice on the DVD, definitely a male voice, said that he would receive said instructions within the next two days. After the DVD finished playing the junior executive extracted it as fast as he could from the player in his computer, handling it as if it was something poisonous.

He knew he would have no choice but to do whatever the instructions that were put forth to him dictated.

And as it turned out he was instructed to allow himself to be picked up by a limousine in front of his place of work after work two nights later.

The junior executive never saw the driver of the limousine because when he got into the luxurious car there was a partition between him and the driver and all the windows on the vehicle were darkly tinted. The way the junior executive knew which limousine to enter on that fateful night was because of the number printed on the side window of the vehicle ...the number which had been in the instructions he had received, via a call on his cell phone. He had to wonder how these people, whoever the fuck they were had been able to gain access to his cell phone number. But he didn't have time to worry about that, the junior executive had more pressing concerns...namely, how to keep copies of the incriminating DVD away from his wife's and work superior's eyes.

When he got into the limousine the driver's voice, a male voice -it sounded like the same voice that had been on the DVD - instructed him to take off his tie and to blindfold himself with it. As he did as he was told the limousine pulled out into traffic. The junior executive was then told to sit back and enjoy the ride. It turned out that the junior executive was blackmailed into starring in porn movies with the emphasis on "Executive Fetish." He was made to have sex with the prostitute named "Candy" and...to his dismay he was made to have sex with men as well.

Wearing just his tie and OTC black socks he was made to allow men to suck his cock while a video camera whirred away and a hand-held camera clicked away as well, capturing stills for the videos.

The junior executive was told by a man wearing a black hood that the videos he had starred in would only be sold to a very *select* group of people...people who had paid for custom-made videos that is...and that the videos would never reach or be available to the general public...as long as he toed the line and continued to do as he was told. When the junior executive reported to the detective now in charge of the case what had been done to him he was told that he was the fifth man to come forward and report such an atrocity being visited upon him. Like him, the other men who had come forward had asked to remain nameless, seeing as their careers in high-profile positions depended upon it. The one thing that all the men who reported being blackmailed said in common was that they had heard the term "Porn to Scorn" being used while they were being filmed having sex with anonymous women...*and men*. It also seemed that the group called "Porn to Scorn" purposely targeted heterosexual men to star in their films... It was said how the people filming and photographing them loved seeing the look of utter humiliation on the straight men's faces as they were made to perform oral sex on other men and even take it up the ass numerous times...

The undercover rookie cop that Sergeant Russo had sent into the camera store as a customer a month or so ago was unable to garner any information that might have led us to make a bust. The way we knew about "Rollies" camera store as a front for the "Porn to Scorn" operation was one of the victims, a high-powered politician had overheard the words "Rollies" camera store being said while he had been being filmed having his testicles licked by two sleazy guys. What we needed was for the rookie cop to somehow become a blackmail victim and then be forced to star in some sort of depraved porn flick, and not be paid for his services. That was the worst part of it for the men who had become blackmail victims of this twisted organization, none of them were paid for their services.

When the junior executive had reported being made to blindfold himself with his tie and then being driven to the location where he became an unwilling porn star he said that his estimate was that the drive had taken close to an hour and a half to two hours, which told me that there was no way they were creating their films at the nearby camera store.

Having plainclothes officers follow the owner of the store home on various occasions had not led anywhere either. One day my shift had just ended and I was driving home for the day, still in my uniform but in a civilian car. Part of my trip home takes me past "Rollies" camera store and as luck would have it I happened to see our decoy cop just coming out of the store. COULD IT BE??? Was it even possible that we had a moll in our ranks??? Fucking fuck, that rookie cop had been no decoy; he hadn't posed as a customer at all, he was what would have been considered a fucking double agent.

No wonder the guy had so adamantly volunteered for the job as a sort of mystery shopper. He had made it sound as if he was a rookie in search of a higher position, he had made it sound so ambitious, and the fools that my superiors were...they had fallen for it. Fuck that, we had all fallen for it. And by falling for it we may have put the victims of this illegal porn ring in even more trouble. I quickly stopped my car at a curb, opened the glove compartment and took out the long-distance lens digital camera that I had bought just recently for my wife.

I was beyond glad at that moment that she had accidentally left the camera in the car. I aimed it at the rookie – his name was Paul Rogan, by the way - and managed to squeeze off enough shots of him to be used as (hopefully) evidence of his involvement in allowing the porn ring to continue to operate. He wasn't in uniform as I was, but just him being at the store after he had been assigned as a decoy for the police department was hopefully enough to incriminate him.

And I knew he was not there on official business at the moment, as technically, he was off-duty. After exiting the store he stood in the establishment's doorway for a few moments and then, lo and fucking behold, Marco Wilson, the owner and the man we suspected of being the head of the illegal porn ring, exited the store next. Wilson stood over six feet. He was built like a goddamned bull, with muscles upon muscles the sizes of boulders. His brown hair was cut in a marine's high and tight style, and the scars on his face were like the highway lines on a roadmap.

His eyes held ice and malice. Seeing the rookie standing there talking to him *and even shaking his goddamned hand* was unnerving. Rogan was a fresh faced young college guy. He had light brown wavy hair and light brown eyes. Wilson towered over him. I squeezed off more shots with my wife's digital camera. It looked like I would not be going home after all; rather I would be heading back to Sergeant Russo with my camera of evidence...

...but then, my plans did a total turnaround. FUCK! The owner of "Rollies" was locking the place up, probably closing for the day. I shoved the digital camera back into the glove compartment as he and Rogan went in opposite directions, to their respective cars. Shit, I bet a week's salary that if I followed Marco Wilson he would lead me right to the place where they were making the illegal porn videos. Showing Russo my evidence pictures would have to wait for the moment...because I knew that if I followed that bastard that I would get even more evidence. I watched as he got into his car and thanked my lucky stars and all the gods in the heavens that I was driving my civilian car; no way could I have followed the guy in a marked police vehicle. As Marco Wilson pulled away in his car I pressed the gas pedal and pulled in two cars behind him.

In my rearview mirror I saw rookie police officer Paul Rogan pulling out in his car, but going in the opposite direction... I licked my lips, gripped the steering wheel tight and when the light turned green I followed Marco Wilson...

We had Wilson's address as a house on the upper west side, but it quickly became apparent we were heading out of Manhattan. I quickly surmised that he had another destination, and more than likely the place where he and his crew made the porn films...

I had no doubt this was the ride the blindfolded junior executive described. I reached into my pants for my cell phone and speed dialed Sergeant Russo's cell number. I wanted to alert him to what I was up to and to let him know the deal with our rookie police officer. I was infuriated to see that my cell phone needed to be charged. And being that I was not in a patrol car, there was no way I could radio for assistance. *Fuck*, I was on my own here; I was on what was called a safari...but unlike other police officers who go on safaris, this was not a safari of my choice. When Wilson reached his destination and I saw what I was dealing with was when I would call for backup... if I could find the means to do so that is. More than likely I could make the bust on my own and then call in backup...just to clean up after my handiwork... I tossed the useless cell phone into the backseat of the car.

Fuck, I saw more than a promotion in the works for this...

I saw myself being a highly decorated and honored police officer, more than likely I would be honored by the mayor and the governor of New York city themselves...

As we drove higher into upstate New York, the traffic thinned out a bit, and I was able to stay one car behind Wilson. There was little danger of I'd wind up getting made. He had no idea who I was after all, and from the distance that I was following him he wouldn't see my uniformed shirt. All he'd see in the rearview was a guy wearing black sunglasses and a dark blue short sleeve button down shirt. I grinned real mean and sinister looking behind my sunglasses and tightened my grip on the steering wheel.

"Oh man Wilson, you have had it, this is your day of reckoning," I mused.

Soon all I could see on the sides of the road was woods. I wondered just how far upstate Wilson had his secret porn ring operation. The junior executive said that the drive had taken a good two hours or so... maybe even more, given traffic conditions I surmised. I glanced at the clock on the car's dashboard and saw that sure enough, I had been tailing Wilson for close to two hours. I was glad that there were still a few other cars on the road along with us, it insured that he had no idea that I was in pursuit. Wilson was one car ahead of me when I saw him turn off the interstate and head for Exit four.

"Okay, looks like we're getting somewhere now," I said softly through clenched teeth.

I eased up on the gas pedal, not wanting the guy to realize that the same car had been tailing him since he'd left the camera store. As I followed him toward a big mansion-like sort of house I thought how my wife was probably wondering where the hell I was and why I hadn't reached home at that point. Fuck, going forward I would make sure to carry my cell phone charger with me at all times. No big deal though, once I made the bust and became a hero, my wife would forgive my having been late getting home on this evening.

It was nearly six thirty PM when Wilson parked in the driveway of an extremely large house. I brought my car to a slow stop along the road. I didn't want to get too close, not just yet at least. It was a warm September day still evening. I watched from a distance as Wilson got out of his car.

"He owns this???" I said out loud, looking at the well-kept hedges and rosebushes surrounding the place.

I lowered my sunglasses a bit to really take in the sight.

The house looked like something that only a famous Hollywood actor could own, or perhaps a Rockefeller or Kennedy. There was no way that the owner of a dinky camera store could possibly own this place, not on his salary.

"Fuck, blackmail must pay real well," I said, pushing my sunglasses back up and cutting the ignition, silencing the car.

Slowly I stepped out, stretching my legs and arms, getting the kinks out after having driven for so long. I wondered how would be my best approach to enter without being seen... But then, to my dismay, that question was answered for me...because, as I stood there with my arms stretched up way over my head and standing on my booted tiptoes, stretching the kinks out, there was no way I could have known that Wilson himself was sneaking up on me from behind...

My duty weapon was fully exposed and displayed on my left side. It was speedily and to my utter shame and dismay easily confiscated from its holster.

"What in the fuck???" I blurted loudly, lowered my arms and whirled around, hell-bent on retrieving my weapon.

But when I turned to face whoever had so easily yanked my gun from its holster I was astounded to come face to face with Marco Wilson himself.

"SHIT!!!!" I roared as he took a few steps back from me, pointing my own gun at my handsome mug. "Wilson...how the fucking fucks..."

"I knew you were following me the whole time, Pig," Wilson laughed, sounding totally sinister and depraved. "As soon as I parked my car I went into the house and made my way behind you through the back door. With all those bushes surrounding the house there was no way you would have seen me..."

SHIT, I had been burned from the get-go...NOW WHAT???

"Wilson, give me my gun, you're making a huge mistake here man..." I said, trying to reason with the guy, making him know very quickly that what he was doing to an officer of the law was illegal and unforgivable at that.

"Actually Officer uh, Harman," Wilson said, looking at my nameplate pinned to my uniform shirt. "It's you who made the mistake by following me here..."

The guy was built like a goddamned linebacker. He had shoulders the size of a doorway, his biceps and triceps were the size of bowling balls and his chest was big enough to eat a meal off of and I gotta say it man, he had tits the size of pointy pencil erasers...all fat and snake-bite sized, FUCK!!! Wilson's abs were a six-pack that was the result of doing a thousand daily stomach crunches. He wore a pair of cut-off jeans that ended just above a pair of big clonky looking black motorcycle boots. Light blue sweat socks stuck out of the tops.

"Look Wilson, I didn't come here alone," I tried. "While we were driving I called for backup and they're already on their way and..."

The guy cut me off in mid-sentence by laughing loud and hysterically, pointing my gun at my head now.

"What the fuck is so funny man???" I seethed miserably. "You are in a shit-load of trouble Wilson..."

"Wrong Officer Pig Harman, *it's you* who is in a shit-load of trouble," Wilson said and clicked my gun.

At the sound of my gun clicking I took two steps back and barked, "Jesus Christ, DON'T SHOOT ME MAN! You kill a cop and you're looking at life in prison, possibly even the death penalty!!!"

When he stopped laughing Wilson said, "You think I don't know that the cell phone you tried calling for back-up on is dead Pig? I saw you toss it in the backseat of your car. The look on your sunglasses covered face was total frustration!"

I clenched my teeth in anger, mostly anger at myself for having been so stupid to not realize that he had been onto me the whole time...and anger at myself now for having been captured this way... Damn, my hunger for a promotion had clouded my thoughts.

With that, Wilson gripped my gun tighter, took two steps toward me and bashed me across the side of the head with it, pistol whipping me...

"ARRRRHHHHHHH..." I cried out. I whirled around stupidly and unbalanced and gripped the top of my car to keep from hitting the ground.

Wilson bashed me across the other side of my head with my gun butt. I sank to the concrete against the side of my car. My head spun and I saw stars as I felt myself being hauled over a huge shoulder and then carried toward Wilson's huge house... my feet dangling over his huge chest, my arms hanging down behind the over-sized, over-muscled thug...

I climbed slowly out of the stupor after Wilson dropped me to the floor like a heap of dirty laundry.

"OHHHHHH GAWD, you bastard..." I sputtered as I pulled myself to my knees, my booted toes pressed against the sleek well-polished un-rugged floor, the palms of my hands supporting me as I pressed them against the floor as well.

"Sexy ass you got there, Harman," Wilson laughed. My butt stuck straight up as I was trying to haul myself to my feet.

"Gee thanks," I said sarcastically and was rewarded with a swift hard kick in that sexy ass of mine from one of Wilson's big boots. "OWWWWWWW!!!"

I landed back on the floor on my stomach...my hands and feet sliding out from under me. I quickly rolled over onto my back, adjusted my sunglasses, and looked up at the man who had become my captor.

"FUCK Wilson, you're sinking deeper and deeper into trouble here," I barked up at him, realizing that I was lying in front of a giant full-length mirror. "Kidnapping a police officer is bad enough, but roughing up that police officer makes your situation all the worse..."

"My situation all the worse, Pig?" Wilson laughed, looking down at me, still pointing my goddamned gun at me. "You have no idea just how bad your situation is about to become..."

That said he kicked me meanly in the ribs, turning me back over onto my stomach...

"HOOOFFFFF..." I grunted miserably. "You fucking bastard..."

"DAMN man, I gotta tell ya Harman, that sexy butt of yours sure does look real fine in those tight fitting uniform britches of yours..." Wilson said, chuckling and then to my mortification he placed a boot on my sexy ass and pressed down hard.

"UHHHHHHH...damn you Wilson, get your mangy foot off me!" I yelled. My ribs and head still smarted.

He slid his boot up and down my damned ass cheeks a few times before taking his foot off me...

"You followed me here, Officer Harman Pig, WHY???" Wilson asked, toeing the side of my ribs with his boot, obviously threatening that he would kick me there again if I didn't reply.

"I know man, *I know* you're running the blackmail porn ring from here Wilson," I sputtered, pressing my palms against the floor, squirming helplessly at that point. "I know you're the head of "Porn to Scorn." And I'm here to prove it..."

"HA!!!! *Here to prove it???*" Wilson laughed down at me, then reached down and grabbed me by the back of the collar of my uniform shirt.

"ACCCHHHHHHH!!!!" I rasped as he yanked me upward by my shirt collar.

"You ain't here to prove shit, Officer Harman Pig!" Wilson barked as my booted toes scraped the floor as I came up cursing and swearing. "Get on your damned booted feet and you'll see why you won't be squealing about this to anyone..."

Once I was on my feet he let go of my collar and I angrily straightened out my askew shirt. When I looked around Wilson was standing in front of me with my gun pointed at my crotch area.

"Fuck man, that really hurt," I said, rubbing my neck and then stood in front of the guy with my arms at my sides, feeling totally useless, stupid and captured.

No one knew where I was, no one knew that I had followed this scum. When I looked around I saw the full-length mirror ...and then, to my utter horror, I also saw a goddamned video-camera set up on a tripod...

...and there was a guy standing behind that camera aiming it at me and Marco Wilson...*and* the camera's red light was on, indicating that it was on "Record" mode... SHIT!!!!

"You're about to star in a movie all your own, Officer Harman Pig," Wilson said to me.

"FUCK, you've got to be kidding Wilson," I suddenly heard myself pleading. "Don't do this! Don't even THINK about doing this!"

"Oh I'm not going to do anything, Officer Harman Pig, I'm not planning to do a damned thing, *you're* going to do it all, and what you're going to do will keep you from telling your superiors about what you found out today..." Wilson said, smirking, still aiming my gun at my crotch.

"What in all fucks are you talking about Wilson?" I asked, clenching my hands into fists at my sides, a feeling of total frustration consuming me. "I won't do anything for you...and..."

"Ah but you will Harman, you definitely and without a doubt will, because if you don't agree to my instructions...

...and agree FAST AND NOW, I will blow your cock and balls away and send you back to your precinct as their first and newest transgender cop," Wilson said and again clicked my gun, this time while it was aimed at my most private and precious area.

"You sick fuck," I muttered, standing there trying my best not to lose it, not wanting to admit I was totally terror stricken.

All my training for hostage situations was going to do me no good here, Wilson was a psycho and a pervert...and he had me in his clutches.

"What do you want from me Wilson?" I asked miserably.

"Like I said, you're going to star in a movie all your own Officer Harman Pig," Wilson repeated. "And I'll be your director…"

I glanced at the mirror he had me standing by and then I glanced over at the guy recording all the action. The implications were awful…

"What, what kind of film?" I asked him.

"We'll call it "Self Stripped Cop," Wilson replied and then he and the guy behind the camera were laughing hysterically.

Fuck, fuck, and triple fuck! They had me right where they wanted me, they planned to make me strip out of my damned uniform…*of all the blasted things*… …and they were laughing at me, cackling, roaring their laughter, it was unnerving, it was fucking mortifying!!!

"Wilson, Wilson, stop this now!" I said sternly, trying in vain to gain control of the situation.

But he and his cameraman simply went on laughing at the trapped and terrified cop…

"WILSON!!!" I roared, demanding to be heard over his infernal laughter. "WILSON!!!"

As if on cue Wilson and his cameraman stopped laughing.

"Jeez Cop, I didn't know you were so anxious to start filming your "Self Strip" epic," Wilson said, looking at me lustfully now.

"Fucker, I'm not ready to start anything," I said and then he raised my gun toward my head.

"Then I suppose we'll just call this movie "Death of a Policeman," Wilson said and even through my sunglasses I could see very clearly down the barrel of my gun.

"NO, NO, Wilson, you don't want to add the murder of a police officer to your roster of offenses!" I blurted crazily.

"Then get into your act, Officer Harman Pig, we're wasting time here. My cameraman is on the clock after all."

"Oh it's okay, I don't mind watching the sexy policeman hem and haw," the cameraman said. "It makes his upcoming performance all the more worth waiting for."

I glanced over at the cameraman, who winked lecherously at me, and then I looked back at Wilson.

"FUCK!! What uh, what do you want me to do?" I asked stupidly.

"Let's start slowly, let's start with you unbuttoning that snazzy uniform shirt of yours and taking it off," Wilson said, grabbing me by my arm and positioning me in front of the full-length mirror, then, he took a few steps back, but kept my weapon leveled directly at me. "But like I said Officer Harman Pig, do it slowly...*real slowly*...make it sexy as hell for your audience..."

I felt a wave of defeat consume me then as I began slowly unbuttoning my uniform shirt, pulled the tails of it out of my uniform britches and bared my well-toned chest and abs.

"Jeez Officer Harman Pig, I gotta tell you, I define myself as a totally straight guy here," Wilson said, grinning and gnashing his fang-like teeth at the sight of my small pointy nipples. "But you sure got nice delectable looking tits for a guy, SLURP SLURP SLURP PIG!!!!"

"Stop it Wilson," I muttered miserably as I dropped my uniform shirt, my pride and joy to the floor at my and his booted feet. "And if you're really smart you'll stop this now!"

Laughing again, the fucking guy stepped on my uniform shirt, smashing my star-shaped badge under his giant clonky boot heel and then kicked my shirt across the room. Seeing my shirt kicked away in the way that Wilson had just done was pretty shitty. In my opinion, a cop's uniform defines him; it's his pride and joy, his mark of satisfaction. And fuck man, Wilson's ugly boots next to my respectable cop boots was just a picture that was all wrong somehow...and my cop boots being in the power of his ugly clonky boots was also all wrong...REALLY WRONG and fucked up for poor me...

"Yeah Cop, fucking Pig, bet your wife loves playing games with those tits of yours huh?" Wilson asked me.

"Leave my wife out of this you bastard, you got me here and that's enough," I seethed through clenched teeth.

"Okay Cop, let my cameraman get some good views of that chest and stomach areas of yours and then I want you to get busy getting those tight and sexy cop britches off," Wilson instructed.

My heart sank deeper than the Titanic.

"Oh fuck man; you really gotta be kidding now, right?" I asked. "Kidnapping a cop is bad enough Wilson, but making him strip at gunpoint is a horse of whole other color...and..."

Suddenly, I saw red as the fucking guy moved faster than lightning and slapped me hard across the face with an open palm.

"OWWWWWWW!!!" I reeled and nearly hit the floor. "You total bastard!!!"

I could not believe that my sunglasses hadn't fallen off my head, that's how hard he had hit me.

With my hand against my cheek I looked up and saw that the fucking guy was rubbing his finger up and down against the trigger of my gun, pointing the goddamned weapon at my forehead now.

"The britches...the fucking britches..." he whispered, sounding lustful and insane at the same time.

WHAT NEXT??? Sadly for me, I would find out all too soon enough.

"Okay, okay man, I'm doin' it, I'm fuckin' doin' it, Wilson, just don't shoot me huh?" I found myself pleading as I began unhooking and unbuttoning and unzipping my police issued britches. "Damn it, man, but this is a shitty ass thing to be doin' to a cop!"

"Oh yeah, fucking sexy pig cop I got here," Wilson said as he now pointed my gun at my sunglasses covered eyes and with my hands and fingers shaking I did his bidding.

"Fuck, what choice did I have really? I didn't want to be filmed stripping out of my cop uniform but I didn't want to be shot dead either buds!

"Do it slow Cop, do it real slow and sexy for your audience," Wilson directed. "Jeez, a real cop doin' a sexy strip tease, I'll make millions off this video!"

"WILSON! You can't mean that, HOLY SHIT!" I railed miserably and in response all Wilson did was chuckle sadistically. "I'll tell you man, no one who ever watches this piece of scummy porn will believe I stripped out of my uniform willingly for you! Everyone who watches it will know I was an unwilling star in this sick flick you got me performing in!"

"WRONG PIG!" Wilson sneered in reply, waving my gun around as I began lowering my police britches to my knees and over my tall boots. "Once I edit this, meaning I'll take out my voiceover and my images and you bitching like a woman it'll be just you strippin', a cop 'Self Stripping' that is!"

"You fucker," I whispered, dropped my duty belt to the floor after I had unhooked it and what Wilson said next sent my heart thundering at what felt like sixty to a hundred miles per fucking hour.

As I stood there with my cop britches down around my knees and over my tall cop issued boots Wilson kicked my duty belt aside with my uniform shirt, took in the sight of my pouch style white briefs, licked his lips in hunger and said, "Okay Pig, get those boots and britches off and then those kangaroo pouch style briefs, you're gonna eat your shorts ...and then you're gonna put those boots back on and jack off for the camera...

"HOLY FUCKING FUCK!!!" I roared, looking up at the guy in disbelief.

"NO, NO fucking way Wilson!!" I prattled on, knowing it was useless. "I won't do it man, I WON'T!!!"

"Now you see Cop, that's the reason I'm gonna make you eat those under shorts of yours," Wilson said, smiling thinly, mockingly. "I've gotten really tired of listening to you complain and whine and state all your clichés. It fucking amazes me that you haven't told me that I won't get away with this, like they used to say in those old-fashioned movies where the so-called hero was captured and set up on some sort of deathtrap."

"Fuck Wilson, but that is the truth, *you won't get away with this*!" I ranted. "Blackmailing those other guys was one thing, but now you've stooped to kidnapping and terrorizing a cop! This won't go over well for you when the time comes!"

"We'll see who it won't go over well for Officer Pig Harman," Wilson said and then he gestured with my gun, down at my boots and I quickly got busy getting them off, followed by my damned underpants.

Fuck, I was going to be socks ass naked in front of the goddamned assailant that I and my cop brothers had been trailing all this time. How's that for sick irony, buds???

Wilson left my boots on the floor between us. As I slid down my underpants, he kicked my britches aside, along with my shirt and duty belt, but not before stomping on them.

"That's no way to treat a cop's uniform Wilson," I seethed.

I felt as if I were being forced to do some sort of sick sexy dance. Wilson looked at me like a lion looking at a deer and I caught his cameraman rubbing his crotch. FUCK!!! Just my goddamned luck that the cameraman had to be some sort of sleazy faggot who obviously got off on cops.

Once I was socks naked I pulled my socks up a bit and then stood facing Wilson. Out of my uniform there was no way I was feeling all that superior anymore. If anything I was feeling totally humiliated, completely violated and entirely powerless. How had this happened??? I was going to have been the one to bust Wilson, and now he had turned the tables and busted me...and this whole scene was only just beginning. Did he really intend to force me to jack off for his camera??? How in all fucks would I get an erection under these circumstances???

"I gotta tell you Cop, you're a natural here," Wilson said meanly, eyeing me slowly up and down, taking in the sight of my nakedness.

As I reached up to take off my sunglasses my sadistic director ordered me to keep them on, saying how it would add to the eroticism of the video as I began to jack off, adding that my big scene would be coming up very soon...as would my cop cock...

"Okay, keep that camera rolling, I want to run through some test scenes here with our budding, *literally* budding star here," Wilson said, grinning. He kept my gun trained on me with one hand as he reached back toward his cameraman with his other.

I watched helplessly as the cameraman reached into a cardboard box that was marked "Props", was next to his camera tripod and brought out a small whip. Fuck, was Wilson planning on whipping my naked ass? If he thought that that was how I was going to lay a hard-on for him and his cameraman, he was sadly mistaken. Kinky as I can get with the wife at times, I'm not into erotic pain, or any pain for that matter. But to my surprise I found my sadistic director handing me the whip.

"What the???" I asked, taking the whip from the guy and looking at him quizzically.

"Pick up your under shorts and stuff them as far into that hole in your face as they'll go, Officer Harman Pig," Wilson dictated. "Then use that whip I just handed you to secure your shorts in your craw..."

Holding the whip in my hand I glanced down at the floor at my underpants and then back up at Marco Wilson.

"You can't be serious Wilson, I've been wearing those underpants since six AM this morning," I said. "And now you expect me to gag myself with them???"

In response Wilson simply took a small step back from me, aimed my gun at my crotch again and pulled the hammer back.

"FUCK!!!" I snarled helplessly. My soft manhood tingled as I dropped the whip to the floor and then bent down to pick up my underpants.

As my cock tingled it felt as if I would piss right there on the guy's clonky boots, FUCK that would have gotten me shot for sure...

With no choice in the matter I picked up my kangaroo pouch style briefs and opened my mouth as wide as possible. God almighty, but this was beyond humiliating!!!

"Crotch section first, Pig," Wilson ordered. "And turn 'em inside out. I want you to really taste your skid marks."

"Bastard, goddamned sick fuck," I whispered miserably and with a quick flick of the wrists I turned my underpants inside out...and began stuffing them into my wide opened mouth.

As I filled my mouth with my underpants Wilson and his cameraman laughed maniacally and mockingly. Seeing as I wanted to live through this ordeal I did my best to fit as much as my underpants into my mouth...

When I was done and just the elastic waistband of my underpants was sticking out of my mouth between my lips I looked at Wilson miserably. With his face all red and tears in his eyes from his having laughed hysterically at me as I had stuffed my craw with my underpants, he gestured with my gun down at the small whip on the floor. Breathing only through my nose, I bent down to pick up the small whip and used it to secure the underpants in my mouth. I caught the cameraman eyeing my big testicles as they dangled oh so enticingly between my thighs. I stood there being filmed as I tied the goddamned small whip over the underpants in my mouth and behind my neck.

"Oh man, nice Pig, real nice," Wilson intoned and I swear I could tell that the fucking pervert was hard as a rock in his ugly pants.

He seemed now to be taking in the sight of my bushy armpits as I secured my underpants into my mouth with the whip he had given me. As I tied the whip over my underpants in my mouth, Wilson reached into his pocket and brought out another pair of white underpants. He dropped them at my socked feet, and as I finished tying the small whip over my underpants filled mouth, I looked at my director questioningly, and not needing to voice my question as to the underpants he had just dropped on the floor at my feet.

"Those under shorts belonged to the last guy we had here that we filmed for blackmail purposes, Pig," Wilson said to me.

I looked at him and shrugged, indicating that I did not understand, nor did I care to know why he was telling me about another man's underpants.

"You should be thankful that I made you gag yourself with your own stinking under shorts, Pig," Wilson said contemptuously. "I was thinking of making you jam the ones on the floor into your pig mouth. The guy that wore them works as a construction worker...and he told me he had worn them for three days straight."

Hearing that I nearly retched, but knew that if I did, I could risk choking to death on my own vomit. Okay, so given the situation I was in, I was thankful that the guy had made me gag myself with my own underpants...rather than the ones that supposedly had belonged to some mangy construction worker...

But then, my thoughts were interrupted when Wilson said, "Okay Officer Harman Pig, get your cop boots back on, NOW!!!"

What was up with all of this??? First he makes me strip down to my goddamned socks, and then he makes me put my goddamned boots back on??? So, once again, because there was a gun, *my gun*, pointed at me *and* because I had no choice in the matter, I did as I was told.

I leaned down, picked up one of my boots and began pulling them back onto my feet. Damn, I felt my testicles dangling provocatively under my ass crack as I pulled my boots back on...and I was sure that the gay sleazy cameraman was checking my balls out again as well...GOD!!!

"Oh man, gonna make you jack off while wearing your cop boots, Officer Harman Pig," Wilson chuckled.

Once my boots were back on my feet, I stood up as straight as possible and looked at Wilson, feeling totally violated, desecrated and dishonored. My arms out in a gesture of confusion, I tried to relate to the guy, as if I were saying, "What now??? Look at me here stripped to my cop boots, sunglasses and gagged??? And gagged with my own underpants at that??? Look at me man, how do you expect me to lay a goddamned hard-on???"

"Oh yeah Officer Harman Pig, now we're getting there," Wilson said.

Looking at Wilson through my sunglasses covered eyes I shrugged crazily and pointed at my soft manhood, trying to relate to him that I wasn't hard...that without being hard I could not jack off and make myself cum.

"RRRRMMMFFFFF..." I snarled at my captor, hoping he understood my message and that he would call this whole thing off and let me go.

But somehow I knew that that just wasn't in the cards.

"Whatsamatter Pig, need a fluffer maybe?" Wilson asked me, sneering. "Damn man, I don't need any goddamned fluffer for me.

Just seeing you all sexy and helpless in those cop boots of yours and eating your under shorts has got me all worked up like you wouldn't believe!"

Somehow I would believe it though I thought to myself...

I nodded my head "NO", that I did not need a fluffer, FUCK, I did not want a fluffer, I wanted out of this heinous situation... A fluffer??? I had heard of fluffers. They were the dudes who helped a porn star lay a hard-on when he might be having difficulty doing just that during the production of a porn movie.

"Damn Officer Harman Pig, anyone ever tell you that your cock hangs down real nice over those ribbed balls of yours?" Wilson asked me. "I've heard it told that when a guy has ribbed balls like yours that his wife loves lickin' them."

I looked at him in total rage and anger as he flicked his tongue around outside his mouth. "That how your wife licks your ribbed balls, Pig?" he asked me.

HOW DARE HE???

"Is that true Pig?" Wilson laughed, reached down and brazenly squeezed the tip of my dangling manhood, sending a shockwave of chills through my body. "Does your wife love licking your ribbed balls?"

In response all I could do was snarl and roar at the guy through my underpants gag...

"Not to worry though, Officer Pig Harman, like you said before, we'll just keep your wife out of this..." Wilson said. "This is your moment in front of the camera after all... and I do have a way to fluff you up in the cock so that this film is memorable..."

Still with my hands out at my sides in a gesture of "But how?" I looked at Wilson as he pointed his gun at my crotch, at my dangling cock...at my ribbed balls...

With that Wilson glanced over at his cameraman and snapped his fingers...

The cameraman set the video-camera on an automatic setting and stepped out from behind the tripod. He stepped over and next to me, looking at me hungrily.

"Do as you're told and let him do what he has to do, Cop," Wilson ordered as the cameraman reached into the deep pocket of the pants he was wearing.

To my horror he brought a capped filled syringe out of his pocket.

As I tried to step away from him he grabbed my upper arm and yanked me back next to him.

"MMMMMMFFFFF???" I railed at Wilson.

"Relax Cop, it's just a hearty dose of Viagra," Wilson said. "Injecting it into you will get you harder faster than if we gave it to you in pill form."

With my eyes opened wide in horror under my sunglasses I looked to my side at the cameraman as he held my arm in his firm grasp, rubbing his thumb almost lovingly but hard over a pronounced vein.

"Man, no need to tie an elastic tourniquet on this cop's arm Marco," the cameraman stated. "Just look at that vein...he's hungry for this stuff..."

As the cameraman then injected the Viagra into my raised vein I stood there shaking in my damned boots...

"Fear not Cop, look at this as an injection for a good erection," the cameraman said as he and Wilson laughed.

When the syringe was a quarter empty, he stopped injecting it into my arm and then, to my further horror and in a lightning quick motion, he injected some of the Viagra into the tip of one of my erect nipples.

"RRRRRRRMMMMMMFFFFFF!!!!!" I screamed behind my underpants gag.

I stood as stock-still as possible with my arms rigid and at my sides as the guy fed me the Viagra through my damned man tit, GOD!!!! When the syringe was empty he took the needle off my nipple and I watched, breathing heavily as he used a couple of cotton cloths to wipe away the small dots of blood that had appeared on my nipple tip.

I swayed and swooned on my booted feet as the fucking fucked up cameraman squeezed my tit through the cotton cloth, sending more chills through me, just as Wilson had done when he had squeezed the tip of my cock...

It didn't take long before I was feeling the effects of the Viagra as it worked its way through my system... Oh man, I felt my manhood tingling...I felt my ribbed testicles tingling...and of course my tits were tingling too...FUCK!!! Wilson had known just how to get me fluffed up and ready to star in his cop epic... Even though I'd had sex with the wife the night before I felt as if I could fuck a dozen women and then some at that moment...but all I would be doing is jacking off...jacking off for a camera with my own police-issued gun pointing at me...

As I stood there starting to feel all worked up and sexy, the cameraman stepped back behind his tripod and Wilson resumed his direction of his unwitting and unwilling actor, me.

"Okay, Officer Harman Pig, let's get this party started right," Wilson said, sounding insanely gleeful as he took me by my arm and moved me directly in front of the full-length mirror. "Grab that cock of yours and start jackin' it slowly..."

I looked at him in utter misery, silently begging him not to make me do this...but when he clicked my gun again and aimed it at my chest; I knew that all bets were off, buds... I grabbed my cock and faced the mirror...and lo and fucking behold, I was hard in a micro-second...

Jesus God on his cross, but my cock looked like a little fire hydrant as I held it in hand and began slowly stroking it. And I have to say; that with just my sunglasses and boots on (not to mention my underpants tied into my mouth with a whip, but okay, what the fuck, I will mention it) I looked somehow really tough and sexy all at the same time. I found myself suddenly stroking myself a tad faster as the camera recorded my action. I panted behind my underpants gag and felt my feet sweating in my boots...

"Slow, Officer Harman Pig, slow," Marco Wilson dictated and I did as he said, not because he was pointing my gun at me...but because slowing down the stroke sure as all hell did feel better than if I were stroking at a fast pace. "Oh yeah, check it out. Pig cop is loving it now..."

I arched my back a bit and gripped my cop cock tighter, really putting my tight and well-muscled ass cheeks on display for Wilson's cameraman...

"HHHHHRRRRRMMMMFFFF, HHHHRRRRRMMMMFFFFF!!!!" I panted from the depths of my throat, the searing sensations of sex coursing through me at what felt like a hundred to a thousand miles per hour.

God almighty, I was one worked up and sexy cop, let me tell you, and at that moment I wanted to cum like nobody's business...

Without Wilson instructing me to do so, I grabbed my cock with two hands. I swayed on my feet and felt like I was marching along to the band. FUCK, but it felt so damned good, buds...

"Shit, check this out man," Wilson said, glancing over at his cameraman. "I don't even need to keep the gun on him anymore. He's totally into this our pig cop here."

The cameraman chuckled and said, "Fuck yeah, Marco, that Viagra does it to them every time..."

No, he didn't need to have my gun trained on me any longer that was for sure. I was more hell-bent on shooting my load than I was at shifting this situation back to my favor at that point. But once I had cum...and once I was no longer Wilson's prisoner, I would have to somehow make it my business to get that video back from him... nobody could ever see it. But at the moment I had more pressing matters in hand, literally. I gripped my manhood tighter yet and stroked slow and hard...

"Look at me, Cop," Wilson demanded then.

"I want your audience to see how turned on and worked up you are at having been turned into a piggy cop, a captured cop, I want them to see how turned on you are by having had every cops' nightmare happen to you."

I looked at him and chewed on my underpants gag, the taste of my cop sweat and skid marks in those underpants were only adding to the sexy revulsion and sleaziness I was feeling, buds. I looked at Wilson and it did not take me much effort to achieve what he wanted. He wanted me looking at him helplessly, desperately, yet aroused all at the same time. For a guy who'd had no training at acting whatsoever, I have to say that I did a damned good job. I felt my toes curling back under my socks in my boots, almost involuntarily it seemed. I stroked my fireplug tighter and then with one hand, my other hand now roaming around in my pubic bush...

I strummed my fingertips over my pubic hairs and somehow it sent more sensations of tingling through me. Never before had I been turned on working my pubic nest. Fuck me hard buds, I could feel my nuts churning away in my sac as well. They were ready to explode a load like never before.

It seemed that Wilson and his cameraman had turned me into a cop porn star. The way my nuts were churning it felt as if they were busily cooking up my sperm, setting it up for a major-sized blastoff.

I found myself looking down at the underpants on the floor between my booted feet.

As I stroked myself harder I wondered how it was that a construction dude, the one that Wilson told me that the underpants on the floor had belonged to, had come to be blackmailed by Marco Wilson. I also wondered what sort of movie the construction worker had starred in for the sadistic director. No way had he held the guy at gunpoint as he was doing to me. No, my gut feeling told me that like the junior executive, the construction worker had become an unwitting pawn for Marco Wilson and his cameraman.

I thought about the construction worker fucking the tar out of some beautiful woman...all while he was unknowingly being filmed. Fuck, what was it about looking at a construction worker's underpants that was getting me so damned turned on all the more???

"Want to sniff them, Officer Harman Pig?" Wilson taunted me and in response I glared at him from behind my sunglasses, snarled into my own underpants gag and stroked myself harder.

I touched the tip of one of my booted feet to the white underpants on the floor and wondered just who the construction worker was...and FUCK it all buds, but Wilson did have a point there. Somehow I wanted to sniff those mangy under shorts.

I stroked my pud some more and thought how if Wilson knew how I got off on sniffing my wife's pussy scented panties at the end of the day how he would no doubt mock me all the more.

"Okay Officer Harman Pig, enough with the pubic hairs," Wilson said meanly. "Maybe for the next movie we'll shave your bush away..."

I looked at him in disbelief. How in all hell would I explain my pubes being shaved off when I got home that night??? If I got home that night that is, I thought miserably, wondering just how long Wilson planned to hold onto me.

"Grab your cock in both hands again Cop," Wilson ordered. "And don't let go until I tell you otherwise...GOT IT???"

I nodded stupidly and did as he said, reached down and with two hands grabbed my throbbing cop cock...

"HHHHRRRRRMMMMFFFFFF..." I panted breathlessly at that point.

Fuck me hard buds, but now, NOW, I really seemed to be into the character that Wilson wanted me to be... I squeezed my butt muscles together really hard, clenching them as I did so and as I gripped my cock again with two hands I arched my back for the camera.

The cameraman moaned in ecstasy behind his camera and I nearly blanched when he told Wilson that they needed to lock this original copy of my debut film in their vault...so that going forward they could use me for future cop videos.

"RRRMMMMFFFFFFF!!!!" I wailed in a mixture of ecstasy and woe.

Use me for future cop videos??? But to my dismay I saw Wilson nodding a most definite affirmative at his cameraman. And then he mockingly said to me, "Welcome to Porn to Scorn, Officer Harman Pig."

I nodded my head "NO" swiftly from side to side and jacked and cranked and yanked my engorged cock. It wouldn't be long now I realized. I could feel my juices boiling over in my nuts. Fuck, I had planned to be the cop who busted "Porn to Scorn." Now I had become their cop star!!!

"Show us that well-toned ass Pig," Wilson then called out to me.

I turned slowly, giving the camera a good view of my sexy tight ass cheeks...

Oh man, as I looked at myself in that mirror and as Wilson pointed my gun at me and as I stood there jacking off I swore to myself over and over that this was not what I wanted, buds.

I DID NOT want to be chewing on my underpants that had been turned into a gag by the man who had captured me and forced me to jack off for him and his cameraman. I didn't want any of this!!! BUT fuck, I was so horned and not reasoning correctly anymore it seemed...because I'll tell you buds, I was about to cum...and cum hard!!! I was literally putting on a sexy show for Wilson's Camera...FUCK, I was gonna shoot a load big enough to choke a horse!!!

It was as Wilson pointed his gun directly at my erect cock and tight feeling ribbed balls that I shot my load. Somehow, the fear that I felt that he was going to blow my manhood away seemed to make me thunder toward orgasm all the more...I've heard it told that sometimes a guy can be what is called "Fear Hard." And trust me on this buds, I was beyond "Fear Hard" at that moment. I was "FUCKING FEAR HARD!"

I shot rope after rope of jizz for Wilson and his cameraman, grunting and croaking from the throat the whole time. I needed to breathe man, and I needed to breathe through more than just my nose. Without Wilson's permission, although he didn't object when I did it, I reached up and undid the bindings over my underpants gag.

Once the bindings were undone I spit my underpants to the floor, licked my dried lips and panted and swore like a captured marine, although in my case I was a captured cop.

"AAAAHHHRRRRRR FUCK, fuck, HOLY FUCK!!!" I seethed as I held my spurting meat-pole with two hands, my jizz sluicing all over me and dripping down my chest area and onto my abs. "DAMN Wilson, that had to be more than Viagra your damned cameraman injected into me!!! I feel like I'm never gonna stop jazzing here, FUCK!!!"

As I shot my load and shot my load (one of the most intense gushers I'd ever experienced, buds) I saw the cameraman rubbing his crotch with one hand while he maneuvered and worked his recording camera over me with the other hand. Wilson meanwhile watched in awe as his captive cop seemed to be like a machine of some sort as I just erupted more and more of my good stuff from my cock slit.

"OOOOOOOHHHHH FUCK WILSON, this is startin' to hurt now!" I panted in a mixture of pain and ecstasy at the same time. "DAMN, I can't seem to stop cumming man!"

But then, a short while later it did eventually taper off. I felt my erection begin to deflate in my hands. As I shot the last spurts of my mess I held my cock in one hand and let what was left of my loads splatter on my leg.

"OOOOOOOOOOOOOOOO..." was the sound that escaped from me as the last of my loads slid down my leg.

"Feelin' good eh Officer Harman Pig?" Wilson asked me and then glanced over at the cameraman.

As I stood there catching my breath I too glanced over at the cameraman.

Along with Wilson I watched as the cameraman took the tape out of the camera, the tape that contained my stripping out of my uniform and then jacking off for Wilson.

"WH-what is he doing man???" I asked Wilson.

Wilson leered at me and held my gun leveled at my spent cock and dangling balls...

"He's just putting your epic in a safe place, Officer Harman Pig," Wilson replied. "That tape will be my insurance that whenever I need a cop in future films you'll come, or cum that is, running at my beck and call."

"NO!!!" I ranted and was ready to pursue and tackle the cameraman as he walked toward the door to the room we were in, carrying the tape of my session with him.

But Wilson reached out, hooked a big hand around one of my upper arms, whirled me like a top, and bent me over so that the top of my head was facing a wall.

"OWWWWWWW, let me go you bastard!" I roared.

As I was about to pull out of the thug's grasp and finally brawl and do battle for my gun and take back control of this situation, I found myself stepping on my underpants with the heel of my boot. Wilson saw this and used it as a golden opportunity. He pushed me hard from behind and sent me sliding like an idiot on my underpants.

"OOOOOOOOHHH SHIT!!!!" I barked and before I could stop myself the top of my head hit the wall in front of me. "HOOOOOFFFF!!!!"

I pressed my hands against the wall and slid down against it...feeling stupid and captured again...

When I climbed out of the stupor that Wilson had knocked me into I found myself in a kneeling position...and to my dismay I was again gagged...but not with my underpants. This time Wilson had gagged me with the underpants that had belonged to the construction worker.

How did I know this? I knew because the taste in my mouth was beyond rancid, buds, it was not the taste of earlier of *my* underpants...FUCK, and Wilson had again used the small whip as a device to secure that construction worker's (whoever the fuck he was) underpants into my craw.

When I looked up at Wilson I was about to pounce but I saw my gun pointing at me yet again... (and that was not all I saw buds, HOLY SHIT) and Wilson barked, "Hands behind you, Cop!" I did as I was told and took in the awful sight before me. As I said,

HOLY SHIT, because while I had been in a stupor Wilson had donned my goddamned uniform.

And to further my feeling of panic and dismay, I saw that my uniform was a good fit for the guy, even though he was built bigger than I was.

"RRRMMMFFFFFF!!!!" I sputtered up at him; the sight of him wearing my attire was just too damned awful and ugly.

"Bet you're wondering what in all fucks I'm doing all gutsied up and wearing your snazzy uniform, huh, Officer Harman Pig?" Wilson asked me as I looked him up and down, realizing that he was barefoot; he had not yet taken my boots, which of course was every thug's fantasy, to steal a cop's damned boots, and right off his feet at that.

I nodded stupidly in reply to Wilson's question...as I looked around for the cameraman.

"Forget it Pig, my cameraman is in the supply room getting supplies for the next shoot, and your tape is safely locked up in my secret vault," Wilson said to me as I kneeled there feeling totally miserable. "Did you honestly think I would allow you to get your mangy hands on it?"

I lowered my head in shame and saw that my cock had returned to a normal state of shriveled and soft...

"Now, I'll be keeping this uniform of yours Pig," Wilson said and I looked up at him in shock. "It's just the thing I'll need for pulling guys over on the highway...when I need new stars for my upcoming films.

And just think, all the guys I pull over and wind up blackmailing will be reporting "Officer Jody Harman" as the cop who abducted them into being blackmailed."

"RRRRMMMMFFFFFFF!!!!!" I roared mightily, the very thought of what he was suggesting totally appalling.

I forgot that he was holding my gun trained at me and in my booted nakedness I lunged at him. But Wilson was ready for me again buds, FUCK!

As I tried to climb to my booted feet the guy grabbed me by one ankle and yanked hard...DAMN!!! I went down a second time, this time on the back of my head...as it hit the floor I had been kneeling on...

"HOOOOFFFFFF!!!!" I grunted again as I was knocked into a second stupor.

When I came around this time I found myself splayed out on my back on the floor...

I quickly hunched myself up on my elbows because it was at that moment that Wilson was doing what most thugs would want to do to any cop they had been lucky enough to capture and use...the fucking guy was stealing my boots!! Actually he had already taken my left boot off my foot, because as I came around and out of the stupor I was watching through my sunglasses as the guy was busily shucking my left sock off my foot.

DAMN, it wasn't bad enough he wanted my boots now, now the fucking guy wanted my stinking socks as well! I had to wonder if he had my pouch style underpants on under my uniform.

"RRRMMMMFFFFFFF!!!!" I railed at the guy as he took one of my socks off me.

"Oh, awake again huh, Officer Harman Pig?" Marco Wilson asked me snidely. "If you don't want another lump on that handsome head of yours I wouldn't try anything stupid at this point. You know how adept I am at snagging you over and over."

In a micro-second it seemed my left sock had been taken off my foot and Wilson quickly and efficiently de-booted my right foot, quickly getting busy helping himself to my other sock as well...FUCK!!!!

"RRRMMMFFFFFFF!!!! RUUUUUUU rasard!!!!" I wailed into the underpants secured in my craw, trying to say, "You bastard!!!"

What he was planning on doing by using my uniform was unthinkable...and there was no way in hell I could stop him! Damn, but I had really fucked this whole thing up big time...

I lay there stupidly watching as Wilson got my socks and boots onto his mangy paws and then began walking away from me...

I sat up, undid the small whip securing behind my neck and spat out the foul tasting underpants, PRONTO!

"WILSON!!! STOP!!! STOP NOW!!!" I roared as I sat up on my knees. "You can't do this man! And besides that...how the fuck am I supposed to leave here all naked and sexy like you got me???"

The fucking guy turned, looked down at me and sneered before he said, "Who said you were leaving, Cop?

Didn't you hear me say that my cameraman was getting supplies for the next shoot? What did you think I meant? While I'm out patrolling in your uniform he'll be filming you here in Part Two of your epic..."

"Fuck Wilson, you can't mean that!! I'm no porn star!!!" I railed at him as he walked toward the door to the room we were in.

"You are now, Officer Harman Pig," Wilson laughed and walked out, leaving me lying there on the floor naked but for my damned sunglasses...

"SHIT!!!" I reeled and quickly got to my feet.

I figured I could find something in Marco Wilson's house of horrors to wear in order to pursue him... I quickly picked up the construction worker's underpants and was about to pull them onto myself...

...but that was when Wilson's cameraman came back into the room, he now pointing my damned gun at me...and wearing what Wilson had had on earlier, his grungy pants, his light blue sweat socks and those socks tucked down into the same style clonky boots that Wilson had been wearing while he had directed me in my "Self Stripped Cop" film.

"The only place those underpants are going, are back into your mouth Cop," the cameraman said and clicked my gun, his finger teasingly squeezing back on the trigger.

Without having to be told to I stuffed the mangy underpants into my mouth and picked up the small whip...

"Oh yeah, got you all to myself this time Cop," the cameraman said as he leaned down over me as I knelt before him in terror and he tickled the bottom of my chin...

Damn, my cop film was going to be a two-parter and I was going to star in the sequel as well...

I watched miserably as Wilson's cameraman got behind his camera and turned it onto "Record" mode...

? The End?

Thinking of my kinky cop buddy...

TITLE: THE GROOM'S FATHER, SERGEANT MAJOR SHELDON

Author: Christopher Trevor and Inspiration from: Jacob

It was a warm and mild Saturday afternoon; a perfect day for a June Wedding. Semi-retired Marine, Sergeant Major Michael Sheldon was with his twenty-four year old blond blue eyed son, Steven, who was about to be married, his son's three ushers, Eddie, Pete and Ronald, and his best man, Adam. They were in the groom's men's preparation room, inside the ritzy and swanky wedding hall, Park Central Banquet Hall.

The forty-five year old bald-domed, blue eyed, rugged Sergeant Major was clad in an olive-colored full military formal uniform, adorned with the rows of medals the corps had had bestowed upon him for his service to his country. He was busting with pride at this occasion of the wedding of his only son to one of the most beautiful young ladies he had ever seen.

"I'll tell you Dad, I'm really starting to feel nervous," Steven, clad in an Armani black tuxedo by Armani and Cole Haan lace-up patent leather shoes, said to his father. He stood rigidly, nearly at attention, as his father stood before him, tying his bowtie for him.

"Nervous about what Steven?" the marine asked in a deep baritone, coarsened by twenty years of barking out orders. "Within the next couple of hours you're going to be marrying the most beautiful, most wonderful, most delightful woman in the world, just as I did years ago where your mother is concerned. Now tell me, what is there to be nervous about?"

"Yeah, really buddy, your handsome dad here is right," said Pete. He was Steven's work buddy, tall, dark haired, dark eyed, and close to thirty. He sidled up next to Steven's dad and playfully, vigorously rubbed the top of the serviceman's bald dome. "What's to be nervous about? It's only marriage after all. And here, check it out, I even rubbed a man's bald head for luck, and that man is your dad. You know what they say, Sergeant Major Sheldon, there's an old superstition that if you rub a guy's bald head it will bring good luck."

"Sure thing Son, but then it would have to be my boy here rubbing this bald noggin of mine eh?" the marine said with a grin.

Steven chuckled along with his usher, Pete, and the other guys. His smile lit up his handsome face as he lifted his hands and clasped his father's big wrists tightly.

"I'm not nervous because I'm going to be marrying Linda, Dad. I'm thrilled about that, I'm nervous about you doing my bowtie."

"HEH, maybe it's me who's a tad nervous after all Son," the marine said. "You're right; I've been working on it for a good five minutes and it's still not right. And after all the formal affairs and events I've attended, I can't seem to do my son's bowtie on his wedding day. Your mother always tied my bowties for me,. But as you can see, for some reason, my uniform ties were never a problem."

Steven smiled as his dad tweaked the firm knot in his own tie, and then slid the black silk bowtie off his son's shirt collar as he placed a palm on his son's cheek.

"I just can't believe it, Steven, you're getting married, I mean, my God, it seems like just yesterday when you were born." Tears nearly filled the marine's eyes, but he quickly choked them back. "Twenty-four years old...my only son...your mother and I are mighty proud of you today Steven."

"Thanks Dad, I appreciate that. But even though I didn't follow in your footsteps and become a marine?" Steven asked. "You know how happy I am working in the world of finance."

"No Steven, you know that never mattered to me," the marine said and held up his son's bowtie. "Want me to try this one more time?"

"Nah, it's okay Dad, I'll get one of these guys to do it before the ceremony in a couple of hours," Steven replied.

"Sure thing Son," the marine said and handed the bowtie to Steven, who draped it around his neck.

With a grin the Sergeant Major leaned down a bit and pointed at his bald dome. His son gave it a good hard rub.

"There you go Son, for good luck, just like your buddy over there said earlier," the marine chuckled.

"Thanks Dad," Steven replied.

"You're welcome," the marine said.

"Dad, could you wait here with the guys?" Steven asked then. "I want to go and check out the room for the cocktail hour, maybe get a quick bite before I take the plunge, if you don't mind that is."

The marine grinned at his son and said, "No problem Steven, just don't accidentally go into the bride and bride's maids preparation room. You do know its bad luck to see the bride before the wedding. And it would be a shame to have bad luck after I just bestowed my bald headed good luck on you, HEH..."

"I know Dad," Steven said. He opened the door to the groom's preparation room, glancing back at his ushers and best man. "You guys okay with me stepping out for a short bit?"

"No problem buddy," said Eddie, a muscular twenty-five year old construction worker. He stepped over to the marine and draped a beefy arm over his shoulder and pulled him close playfully. "We'll keep your soldier boy dad company; some champagne should calm his nerves…"

All the men laughed good-naturedly as Steven closed the door behind him.

"And for the record there Eddie, I'm a semi-retired marine, not a soldier boy. There's a difference between a marine and a soldier, a big effing difference," Sheldon said as Eddie guided him toward the large table where the drinks were all set up for them.

"Sir, yes Sir and OOH RAH," Eddie said loudly and the marine grinned from ear to ear at Eddie's hearty response. "Now, Adam, seeing as you're the best man to this marine's son, you may have the honor of pouring him a glass of champagne."

"Coming right up," Adam, a twenty-eight year old real estate broker with light brown hair, brown eyes and a short beard said as he picked up a glass and an open bottle of bubbly.

"Thanks guys, I appreciate this, I guess I really am nervous," the marine said. "I mean, Steven was the only kid his mother and I had and…

…well, now he's getting married and leaving the house and…well, it's enough to make any parent nervous I suppose…"

"Not to worry, Sergeant Major, you'll be fine," Eddie said, pulling the marine closer to him and holding him tighter at the shoulder. "I tell you man, Steven is real lucky to have a marine for a dad. I wish my dad had been a serviceman. I love uniforms, the shiny black shoes, the medals, the whole fucking package Sir, OOH RAH."

"It's really no big deal, Son," the marine said, a bit taken aback as to the way Eddie had him in his manly grip, but somehow enjoying it nonetheless, just as he had somehow enjoyed it when Pete had taken liberties in rubbing his bald dome. "I just wanted to serve my country, that's all, plus my dad had been a marine, and my grandfather, and his dad…"

"Here you are, Sir," Adam said, stepping in front of Sheldon and handing him a tall glass of champagne. "Down the hatch, as you, I think marines say."

"That we do. Son, that we do," the marine laughed, as he took the glass from Adam and chugged down a big swallow.

"Good, Sir?" Eddie asked, his hand having moved up to and behind the back of the marine's big bull-sized neck, squeezing it tight, kneading it.

"Yeah, very good Son," the marine replied, turning his head to look at Eddie. He realized that their mouths were scant inches away from each other's. "Say uh, *what all* goes on here, bud?"

And was that a hand the Sergeant Major felt, brushing across his rear end as Adam stepped back to the table?

"Just wanting to serve our country, Sir, that's all," Eddie said and as he spoke his lips grazed the Sergeant Majors. "As you said Sir, just want to serve...OOH RAH..."

"Well I'll be damned boy, I swear, the gateway to your face is close enough to fucking kiss me if you chose to..." the marine said through quivering lips. Eddie's big hand caressed the back of his neck and held it so tight he could not move his face away from the other man's.

"Yes Sir, close enough to *kiss* you, Sergeant Major, ain't that something, eh?" Eddie said with a lust-filled grin. His lips again grazed the marine's.

Then, to the Sergeant Major's total shock and utter surprise, Eddie cautiously moved in even closer, testing the waters so to speak, and when he sensed no resistance from the serviceman he pressed his lips hard against the marine's...

"GRRRRMMMFFFF..." was the sound the marine made as Eddie's mouth pressed down harder and harder on his.

...and the Sergeant Major found himself, instead of pulling away from the other man's brazen kiss, responding in kind, forcing his long tongue into the usher's mouth. The taste of expensive champagne on the marine's mouth seemed to egg Eddie on all the more. They kissed each other harder and with more determination. Adam stepped in front of the two men and began tugging on and undoing the marine's uniform tie.

"What in all..." the Sergeant Major said huskily as he peeled his lips off Eddie's and saw what Adam was doing.

"Just relax Sir," Adam said softly as he undid the Sergeant Majors tie. "Like you said, you never had a problem doing up your uniform tie."

"NOPE, never did at that," the marine replied, sounding dumbstruck over what was happening at the moment, but making no move to stop Eddie or Adam in their endeavors.

Once the tie was off Adam quickly and busily unbuttoned the marine's uniform jacket.

"Lots of medals you're sporting here, Sir, I'll bet you earned them all vigorously," Adam said with total respect, he leaning over and licked and kissed some of the medals.

"Holy shit on a shingle...what all are you mugs up to here???" the marine croaked, but he did not resist as Eddie palmed the top of his head and guided his mouth back to his.

"Open wide. Sergeant Major," Eddie said demandingly and the marine, without hesitation, complied, opening his mouth real wide.

This time Eddie meanly spit two wads of saliva into the marine's mouth, ranted in the serviceman's face, "Fuckin' sexy soldier boy you are, Sir, now, tell me, who's a horned dog marine?" Before the sergeant major could reply. Eddie spit two more wads of saliva into his still wide open mouth.

Then, the marine said, "I am Son, I'm a horned dog marine," and Eddie quickly clamped his mouth down on the sergeant Majors and sucked his wads of saliva back out of the marine's craw.

"Fucker, told you I was a damned marine, a fucking leatherneck," the marine began when Eddie stopped sucking his mouth for the moment, but Eddie quickly cut him off in mid-sentence by clamping his lips down again on the serviceman's waiting lips.

At the same time, Adam was unbuttoning the marine's uniform shirt. His jacket had been removed by the usher named Pete.

His half empty glass of champagne had been taken from him as well and placed on the nearby table. Ronald, the third usher, a muscle bound handsome brute who worked as a personal trainer in a gym, was hunkered down in front of the occupied marine and was slowly undoing the marine's belt. The sounds of kissing, slurping and slobbering filled the air.

"M-my son, he'll be back soon and..." the marine began as Eddie stopped kissing him.

"Not to worry, Sergeant Major, the door is locked," Adam said, stepping close in front of the marine, taking in the sight of his hairy colossally muscular robust pecs.

He grasped the sergeant majors VERY pronounced pink nipples in his thumbs and first two fingers of each hand.

"So if anyone comes they'll have to knock before they can get in here..." Adam said as he tweaked, twisted and pinched the marine's nipples.

"G-good deal Son, UHHHHHHH, jeez, for a guy I always had real sensitive nubbins," the Sergeant Major huffed, and then it was Adam's turn, he leaned in real close and clamped his mouth down on the marine's, twisting the serviceman's nipples at the same time.

"RRRRHHHHH…" the marine growled as he was kissed and his nipples were twisted, his mind awhirl and totally befuddled over this somehow delightful turn of events… just before his son's wedding.

The Sergeant Major felt his zipper being pulled down. He stamped one foot as tears of ecstasy filled his eyes and then felt his proud and massive sized manhood and kiwi sized testicles being extracted from within the confines of his pants…and then… Oh God and OOH RAH. Those pants were being slowly and methodically pulled down his stout legs, revealing his olive colored marine issued briefs…briefs he would not be wearing for long, as fingers gripped the sides of those briefs and slowly pulled them down. The three ushers and best man stole sniffs and licks on the marine's briefs… revealing his gargantuan erection and low hanging testicles, OOH RAH…

A few moments later the Sergeant Major was standing nearly at attention, clad now in only his black OTC silk wedding style socks and well-shined patent leather lace-up military issued dress shoes. Eddie and Adam stood at his sides, each of the men taking turns kissing him long and hard, tonguing his mouth, trailing their tongues over his healthy gums, each of them twisting one of the marine's nipples hard and tweaking and rolling the tips, teasing the bejesus out of the serviceman, making his bald head spin…

…while at the same time, at his lower area, Pete and Ronald were hunkered down in front of the sergeant major and licking his nuts, sucking them alternately, swelling them up to the size of cum filled golf balls, and then taking turns sucking the Sergeant Majors huge marine-sized steely baby maker, eating the pre cum from the tip as it oozed…

"JEEEEEZZZUSSSS, fucking guys, best buddies my son ever had," the marine groaned from deep in his throat when his mouth wasn't being kissed or slobbered in.

At the marine's crotch Pete and Ronald caressed the serviceman's iron-like calves, leaned down to kiss his marine style shoes a few times, licked his calves, playing with his socks, paying him true reverence for his services to his country, and then licked and kissed their way back to his cock and balls, kissing his legs and thighs as well as they went…

"AWWWWWWW OOH RAH, no one will believe this shit," the marine groaned in ecstasy.

Then, Eddie and Adam leaned down and each of the men took one of the marine's jutted up nipples into their mouth, slurped hard on them, chewed on them, sucked them and licked the very tips. At the same time they reached behind him and cupped one each of his hard muscled butt cheeks in their hand, kneading and squeezing the marine's butt cheeks as if their lives depended on it... ...while at his crotch Pete and Ronald continued their services at the marine's skyscraper erection and juicy balls... caressing his calves at the same time...

"YUHHHHHH, fucking dudes, YEAAAHHHH, fuckers, suck my marine sized tits, that's it you fucking mugs, OOH RAH, suck my cock, lick my goddamned balls, squeeze my hairy ass, show me the goddamned respect I deserve..." the marine growled and swore in his baritone. "No one would believe what occurred before my boy's wedding...no one...YUHHHHHHHH..."

The marine threw his head back, raised his muscular arms and caressed the backs of Eddie's and Adam's heads and necks as they sucked at his nipples with the ferocity of two jacked up vacuum cleaners...

"OOOOOHHHH yes, fucking mugs, getting me all horned up here," the marine stated. He saw how hard his manhood was and how it twitched due to the service that Pete and Ronald had bestowed on it. "Feastin' on me that's what you guys are doin', fuckin' feasting on me, OOH RAH..."

Then Eddie and Adam suddenly reached under him and at the same time Pete and Ronald lifted the marine's muscular legs...and seconds later the serviceman was airborne and being carried to the table...

"OOH RAH, strong fuckers you boys are, what all you got in mind for your serviceman now, HUH???" the marine said throatily as he was placed atop the end of the table on his ripped and muscular back, his legs dangling off the end of it. "Fucking mugs..."

A few moments later the marine's legs were high in the air, being held with the bottoms of his shoes looking up at the ceiling by Adam, who was straddling the serviceman's torso atop the table. Adam spread the marine's legs out, holding tight to the serviceman's calves, revealing his bunghole for the other three men in the room. The three men took in the sight of the marine's backdoor as if Adam were opening a present for them.

"OOH RAH, like I asked already, what all do you mugs have in mind for me next huh?" the marine asked and when he looked up he saw that Adam's hard, extensive and very thick virility was sticking out of the fly opening of his tuxedo pants, along with his big hairy balls.

"AWWWWWW JEEZ...and would you look at that??? Ain't that just so fucking pretty?"

Suddenly, Adam's eyes crossed and he gasped and grunted loudly as the marine under him lifted his head and slurped the best man's erection into his mouth, while his balls rested atop the marine's nose.

"YUHHHHHH...oh fuck, oh shit you guys, this goddamned jarhead is sucking my fucking cock," Adam lambasted breathlessly. "Feels so top drawer you guys..."

As his cock was sucked and his balls sniffed heartily, Adam leaned forward and trailed his tongue up and down and up and down one of the marine's silk socked calves, pecking them with kisses, licking them and then kissing them some more... Adam rocked himself up and down in a steady motion as the marine sucked him harder and sniffed his balls with total gusto.

"UHHHHH, fuck yeah you sexy leatherneck, fucking jarhead, suck my cock," Adam whispered breathlessly and ran his hands up the marine's calves and to his socks and shoelaces.

Adam rocked up and down, thrusting his cock in and out of the marine's mouth and unlacing the serviceman's shoelaces at the same time. Adam worked the marine's shoes off his feet and dropped them to the floor, but not before deeply inhaling the scent of leather and marine sock and feet sweat from inside each one, while at the same time the other three men in the room had extracted their rage hard cocks from their tuxedo pants...

"Oh yeah you guys, this is the pussy of the moment," Eddie chuckled, hunkered down at the marine's gaping pink bunghole, hacked up a goodly amount of saliva and spit it directly into the serviceman's backdoor.

"OOOOO, fucker you are Eddie, that's one hell of a way to refer to a marine's shit chute," said the marine with his legs in the air. He quickly glugged Adam's cock back into his mouth and resumed servicing it.

Seconds later, Eddie, Ronald and Pete were all hunkered down on their haunches in front of the marine's on display asshole and were taking turns spitting into it, prodding it with their fingers, teasing the utter fuck out of it, and eating their saliva back out of the serviceman's hole, while at the same time slurping, licking, lapping, and even sucking at the jarhead's ass walls.

"AWWWWWW FUCK, FUCKING FUCK, this is all too much now, you goddamned mugs treating my backdoor like a danged pussy," the marine grunted, the tip of Adam's cock against his lips as he spoke, Adam's big cum filled balls resting all moist and juicy on his nose. "And look at this fucker above me, while I suck his damned pud he licks and kisses my silky socks...OOH RAH..."

"Less talk and more suck, Sergeant Major Sir," Adam laughed and slid his erection back into the warm confines of the marine's craw. "MMMMM...oh fuck yeah..."

Then, once the marine's backdoor was as wet as a duck's bottom, Eddie, Pete and Ronald stood up, their massive erections sticking out of their tuxedo pants.

"Okay guys, his son may come back any minute now, let's make this count for this proud sergeant major," Eddie said and stepped up close to the marine and slid his cock slowly inside the serviceman inch by inch.

"MMMMMFFFFF..." the marine uttered around Adam's cock in his mouth, and his eyes crossed for a moment or two, as Eddie's high-rise slowly entered him and stretched his ass walls.

Sergeant Major Sheldon gripped the sides of the table he was laying on, curled his toes back under his sheer socks, and sucked Adam's cock with more gusto as he felt his ass walls being spread wider and wider to accommodate Eddie's massive girth...

"Oh fuck, he loves it you guys, or as he says, you mugs," Adam laughed. "Fuck, I'm getting close, gonna make this marine eat my dick slime."

"RRRRMMMFFFF..." the marine with the mouthful of cock blubbered and gripped the sides of the table tighter yet as the rest of Eddie's cock filled his ass-funnel and he was forced to deep-throat Adam's cock at the same time.

Eddie thrust in and out of the Sergeant Major's hole, using his calves as handles to balance himself, and stealing sniffs of the marine's socked feet at the same time. The scent of jarhead sock sweat caused him to ram the marine's most private crevice harder and harder with each thrust.

"AWWWWW fuck yeah Sergeant Major Sheldon, real nice tight and inviting hole you got here, your pussy hole is simply sucking my cock back in every time I thrust it out," Eddie seethed, held tighter to the marine's socked calves and buried his cock deeper inside the serviceman.

Then, Eddie extracted his hard pre-seeding cock from the marine's hole, stepped aside and Pete went next. He gripped the serviceman's calves and began sliding his cock inside him...and then, a few minutes later Ronald did the nasty in the marine's hole, fucking him with the force of a jackhammer it seemed...

...and then Eddie was back for round two...all of the ushers fucking the marine over and over until they shot their pent-up loads inside him, each of them filling his sweet opening with their nectar.

"GGGRRRRFFFF..." the marine snarled as Adam then shot his load, right down the serviceman's throat...

As the marine swallowed and swallowed Adam's load and as his asshole was made to swallow the loads of the ushers, his bald head spun and his mind wandered back to his earlier days in the service when he was still a sergeant, and when he and two lance corporals used to have some private fun in his office...

As he remembered and as he was fucked and as he swallowed cum, his cock stiffened all the more and he could see it in his mind as if it were happening right this moment...

The Sergeant was in his private office, it was right after he had worked his platoon of recruits through a harrowing session of Basic Training out on the field. Out of his fatigues, combat boots, showered and clad now in his dress uniform, the robust and ruggedly handsome sergeant looked up when he heard the knock on his door.

"Yeah, come in," he called out, sounding as brusque and as authoritative as possible, but knowing that with what was about to occur he was not to be the man in charge... *at least not at this moment.*

Two handsome and muscular lance corporals stepped into the sergeant's office, both of them also wearing their dress uniforms and closing and conspicuously locking the door behind them. They looked across the room at the sergeant, saluted him, and stood instantly and rigidly at attention.

"You sent for us, Sir?" the first lance corporal asked, a young, well-built twenty year old blond boy from Nebraska.

"I sure as shit did guys," Sergeant Sheldon replied with a sly looking grin on his face as he took a pair of handcuffs and a black cloth silk blindfold out of the top drawer of his desk. "Okay you mugs, strip down. I think you should know the drill of this routine by now."

The two lance corporals shouted a hearty "Sir, yes Sir!!" in unison and quickly stripped out of their uniforms, putting on a show for their sergeant. When they were totally stripped the first lance corporal said, "Now it's your turn, Sergeant Sheldon Sir." The two lance corporals stepped to the sergeant's sides and began helping him out of his uniform, beginning with undoing his necktie...

Within a few scant minutes the horned up Sergeant Sheldon was naked except for his black calf length dress socks. The serviceman's big cock stuck out hard, almost as if it were pledging allegiance to the two underlings he had submitted to. The two lance corporals locked his hands behind him in his own handcuffs; each of them clicked one of the wrist manacles shut and together they blindfolded him. Without a word the sergeant then spread his muscular legs wide and stood balanced before his two underlings. The two lance corporals then proceeded to run and trail their hands over the sergeant's huge rock-hard chest and at the same time they squeezed and teased his colossal nipples.

"Outside of this office you may be in charge, Sergeant Sheldon Sir, but in here *we are*," *chuckled* the second lance corporal, a lanky five foot nine brown haired, brown eyed twenty something year old kid from down south, as he tugged on the sergeant's earlobe.

Sergeant Sheldon smiled behind his black silk blindfold and the two lance corporals took a few sucks each on his bulbous nipples, flicking their tongues over the very pointed tips.

"Get busy you two," Sergeant Sheldon suddenly barked.

The first lance corporal knelt behind the handcuffed and blindfolded sergeant, gripped his ass globes and spread them wide and began lapping and licking the serviceman's hole, slurping the sergeant's ass chowder greedily down his throat. The second lance corporal sucked heartily at the sergeant's nipples, working them hard and alternately.

"OOOOOHHHH OOH RAH, yeah, fucking A you mugs," Sergeant Sheldon panted. "All I could fucking think about today out on the physical training field was having you two in here eating my mangy manly ass, servicing my big marine sized tits and then playing FUCK with you guys!"

The sergeant's manhood grew harder and harder with each passing second.

The first lance corporal slapped Sergeant Sheldon's ass globe a few times while his face was buried in his stinking crack.

"MMMMMM oh yeah, OOH RAH, lick my hole, suck my tits!!" Sergeant Sheldon demanded. "FUCK YEAH!!! It's a fucking crying shame I can't get my wife to do these things for me...and while I'm handcuffed and blindfolded at that, at your fucking mercy boys...OOH RAH..."

As the two lance corporals worked him over Sergeant Sheldon's cock became hard as steel, his testicles hung down low like two lemons in his hairy sac...

The second lance corporal then leaned over the desk and spread his legs apart, revealing his pink and eager bunghole... The first lance corporal guided the blindfolded Sergeant Sheldon behind him...

"Okay Sergeant Sheldon, Sir, his ass is right in front of you," the first lance corporal said, squeezing his sergeant's rock-hard ass globes, loving the feel of them.

Sergeant Sheldon thrust forward and pushed his steely erection into the second lance corporal's ass slowly, inch by inch, the tip of his cock kissing the kid's rosebud and then he plowed in up to his balls, fucking the lance corporal's most clandestine crevice.

"OH YEAH!!" the second lance corporal gasped at the intense invasion. "Fuck me Sir, fuck me with that gargantuan cock!! OH YEAH!! OOH RAH SIR!!!"

As Sergeant Sheldon fucked the second lance corporal the first lance corporal continued licking and lapping at the sergeant's asshole.

"OHHHHHH FUCK yeah!!" Sergeant Sheldon croaked throatily.

It went on and on like that for a while, Sergeant Sheldon pounding hard on the second lance corporal's ass with his big cock wedged deep inside the kid while the first lance corporal feverishly drooled in the robust sergeant's ass and slurped it back out again and again, driving the handcuffed and blindfolded serviceman crazy.

"Oh yeah, going to fill your hot ass with my marine-sized load of cum!!" Sergeant Sheldon grunted. "OOH RAH!!"

Sergeant Sheldon then shot his hefty load and the second lance corporal felt the marine's warm thick creamy fluid fill his hole.

"OH YEAH, FUCK YEAH, yes Sergeant Sheldon Sir!!" the second lance corporal gasped and panted as Sergeant Sheldon thrust like a madman inside him, grunting like a real marine.

Next, the two lance corporals sat Sergeant Sheldon up on his desk. The spent sergeant took heavy and deep breaths as his two underlings began licking one of his big feet each and jacking themselves off at the same time. Sergeant Sheldon was still handcuffed and blindfolded.

"OH YEAH, fucking A, lick my stinking feet, love having homage of all kinds paid to me!" Sergeant Sheldon snorted. "Suck on my smelly socks, that's it you mugs..."

With a few minutes the sergeant's black dress socks were soaked with saliva, then, the first lance corporal removed the sergeant's blindfold, and the marine watched as the two lance corporals shot their loads all over his feet.

"Damn, ain't that so pretty guys, your thick white cum all over my black power socks, OOH RAH," the marine grunted.

"Damn, no one on this base has it better than I do," he then said to himself behind a fiendish grin. "Look at these two, licking my goddamned socked feet like two obedient puppies..."

A short while later the three men were dressed. The two lance corporals left Sergeant Sheldon's office and the marine put the handcuffs and blindfold back in his desk, a smile of true contentment on his handsome face...

"HEH makes their day to use and abuse a superior officer," the marine said aloud.

Sheldon's mind was propelled back to the present, as Adam slowly slid his spent cock out of his mouth and let go of his socked calves. Sheldon sat up on the table, his muscular legs dangling off the end.

"Fucking mug, you're the ringleader here, bud, turned my hole into a pussy," the marine grunted at Eddie, reached out and grabbed the usher by his spent cock and gave it a hearty twist. "I'll make it your job to get me off..."

Seconds later Eddie was hunkered down over the marine's muscle pipe, sucking it like a madman, the palms of his big hands pressed against the table.

"OOH RAH feels awesome to have my hard cock sucked after being fucked six ways from Sunday by you mugs," the marine said with a grin. "FUCK, its not just any mugs that I allow to fuck me, usually I'm the one doing the fucking...DAMN, getting close already Eddie..."

As Eddie sucked the marine's cock for all he was worth he cupped the sergeant major's balls in one hand.

"AHHHHH nice, real nice, fondle those marine sized balls of mine buddy," the marine gurgled. "I'm about to feed you a nice helping of jarhead slop."

Eddie felt the marine's cock throbbing in his craw, he sucked it harder and the serviceman threw his head back in total and sheer ecstasy...

"OOH RAH, OOH FUCKING RAH you mug, I'm gonna shoot a load big enough to choke a goddamned horse!!" the marine seethed, palmed the top of Eddie's head and forced the usher to chow down real heartily. "AWWWWWWW YEAH, fucking marine loving dudes you guys are...FUUUUUCCCCKKKK..."

Sergeant Major Sheldon rocked up and down atop the table as he seemed to cum and cum, forcing every drop of his good stuff down Eddie's throat, the other ushers and best man all suddenly taking turns rubbing the marine's bald head and stealing deep kisses from him...

When the marine was spent his cock slid out of Eddie's mouth, he lowered his head to face forward...and to his total SHOCK saw his son Steven standing in front of him at the end of the table he was seated on...

"Dad?" Steven said as he took in the sight of his marine father clad in just his tall black silk wedding socks.

"AWW fuck, Steven, look son, I can explain, we uh, we thought the door was locked and we just got into some playful shenanigans and..." the marine began, but then saw his son's face light up like a Christmas tree.

Eddie and Adam each grabbed one of the marine's socked calves, yanked him to his back again on the tabletop and hoisted his legs up, up, up...and spread them as wide as possible...

"ARRRRRRHHHHHHH oh my fucks, oh my fucking fucks!!!" the sergeant major was growling seconds later as his only son, his tuxedo jacket and shirt sleeve rolled up on his arm to the elbow and was slowly inching that arm into his dad's rectum. "Fisting your old man...what a good luck thing to do before you get married son..."

When his son's fist hit home the marine shot a second whopper of a load...without his pride and joy even being touched or sucked this time, all over his massive sized chest, pecs and nipples...

"OOH RAH, OOO FUCKING RAH..." the marine snarled and the best man and ushers all applauded and whooped it up for their groom buddy and his marine dad.

Later, Steven, his marine dad and mom, his three ushers and best man were all in the reception room as the young man and his bride took their vows. The marine, all done up again in his uniform, his wife on his arm, both of them looking prouder than proud as their son got married, looked over at Eddie and the other two ushers and winked, a knowing look passing between the men...a look that seemed to say, "See you again in the preparation room after the wedding...

/The End/

PS: A special thanks to my online marine buddy for the fisting idea...

TITLE: GREG GREGG'S WHIRLPOOL JACUZZI

Author: Christopher Trevor and inspired by the executive style followed by gunged style of my new buddy, Greg Gregg

It had been a hectic day at work that day, no, fuck that, it had been a hectic *week* that week at work. Problem after problem, computer system kept going down, excuses from IT after excuses, customers calling one after the other because they couldn't log into our company's website to check on their orders…DAMN, was I glad it was Friday buds.

As I rode home on the crowded train, grateful to whatever gods were watching over me that I had been able to get a seat, I dozed a bit and thought about just getting home, having a quick light dinner and a beer and hitting the sack. No TV this Friday night, I was too damned wrecked and stressed. Plus my wife was out of town on a two-week business trip for the company she worked for, we had no kids, so lo and fucking behold, I had the whole house to myself for the upcoming weekend.

I got off the train around 6:30 PM and hoofed the four blocks from the station to my one family house in the middle of a quiet street called "Sodden Avenue." Clad in a navy blue suit, a white button down stiffly starched collar shirt, a silk burgundy power tie and highly shined black lace-up wingtip shoes, I made my way down the avenue.

Gripping my black leather attaché case in one hand I waved politely and said hello to neighbors who happened to be sitting out on their porches or on the other side of the avenue, relaxing in their backyards.

When I got to my house I reached into my suit jacket pocket for my keys and as I was about to slide the key into the front door's lock, I heard voices coming from my backyard, *or,* to be more precise, I heard voices coming from the wooden enclosure in my backyard where my wife and I had had a whirlpool Jacuzzi installed.

"What in all fucks?" I whispered, turned away from the front door and walked quickly to my backyard and toward the wooden enclosure.

My wife and I had had the enclosure built around the whirlpool Jacuzzi for the obvious reasons of privacy. We always kept it padlocked when we weren't home. Now, to my total chagrin I saw that the padlock had *literally* been sawn off the door. And not only did I hear voices, male voices that is, coming from within the enclosure, but I also heard the sound of the water jets turned on and splashing coming from the whirlpool Jacuzzi.

"What in all hell is going on in there?" I said out loud, as I yanked the door of the enclosure opened and stepped inside.

I took a few more steps into the wooden enclosure, slammed the door closed behind me and saw four of my neighbors, Dennis, Howard, Alex and Ronald, all sitting in the whirlpool. They had beer mugs and coolers set out on the sides of the deck that the whirlpool Jacuzzi was mounted on and I even smelled cigar smoke in the enclosure.

I surmised that all the men were totally nude, seeing as I saw clothing stacked up on the floor, INCLUDING goddamned stinking pairs of briefs and mangy looking pairs of sweat socks, JEEZ! And I had been right, *I had* smelled cigar smoke, seeing as there were a few ashtrays on the floor of the deck as well, with mounds of smoked and half-smoked stogies in them.

"WHAT THE FUCK IS THIS???" I shouted, stepping up onto the deck and glaring down at my neighbors as they were sitting in a circle in *my* whirlpool, obviously enjoying *themselves*.

"Oh, hey there Greg, how're you doin' there guy?" Alex, a guy in his mid-thirties, single, who was built real lankily, curved and sort of muscular, with blond hair and mischievous looking blue eyes, said upwards to me, smiling from ear to ear.

"What do you mean *how am I doing???*" I barked down at the guy, able to see him in all his damned nakedness as he sprawled there in the Jacuzzi, AND I mean ALL his nakedness, if you know what I mean. "What I should be asking is *what in all hell are you four doing here???*"

"What does it look like we're doing bud?" Ronald, a burly weight-lifting type of guy with brown hair, brown eyes and in his late twenties asked me in reply. "We're simply enjoying the whirlpool."

"Yeah, I have to say that this was a great idea that you and your wife had, bud," Dennis piped up from where he was seated at the far end of the whirlpool. He reached for a mug of beer that was on the deck next to him and chugged down a sip. "Installing a whirlpool Jacuzzi in your backyard was really an executive decision on your part, bud."

Dennis was a married dude, in his thirties like Alex, but unlike Alex his blond hair was a dirty blond, he had greenish eyes and he was built more on the average side.

"Bullshit, this is private property, and from what I see outside you guys sawed the padlock off the door of my enclosure," I spouted angrily and stepped closer to the Jacuzzi.

"Well how else were we supposed to get in here to use the whirlpool, bud?" Howard asked me snidely.

He, like Ronald, was on the muscular side, but not an avid weight-lifter. He had brown hair and brown eyes, and was in his late twenties, and married - his wife was pregnant with their first child.

"That's not funny Howard, not funny at all, and stop calling me *'bud'*, all of you," I shouted now, beyond angry at their outright impertinence. "At the moment I'm really not feeling like your *bud.*"

"Hey come on, relax Greg, we'll replace your padlock," Ronald said. He reached out of the whirlpool with one big ham-sized hand, under the pant leg of my left-sided suit trousers, and tightly gripped my navy blue nylon socked ankle. "And from the way you're carrying on, *bud*, it's obvious you've had a stressful day, probably a stressful week."

As he held my socked ankle tight I could not help but look down at my feet in horror, OH NO, he couldn't be thinking what I thought he was thinking, could he??? I mean, unlike my four prankster neighbors, I was fully clothed, not even in swim trunks for heaven's sakes, not meant to be taking a dip in the Jacuzzi at the present moment.

"Yeah, lots of stress isn't good for a guy Greg," Alex quickly chimed in and before I could pull my left foot out of Ronald's grasp, Alex had me by the right foot, namely, he had me by my right ankle, oh the horror. "From the look of things *you* need a good dip in here with us...and some other festivities as well...*bud...*"

With that, Alex and Ronald began tugging on my ankles, yanking me forward, tottering me closer and closer to the jettisoning whirlpool...

"G-GUYS, no, FUCK, let go of my goddamned feet, NO, what in all hell are you..." I began, my arms swinging uselessly at my sides, my attaché case still in one hand. "OH HOLY FUCK, NO, NO!!!"

I lost my balance and went careening face-first downward, plunging into the whirlpool Jacuzzi, suit, shoes, attaché case and all.

"And SPLASH DOWN!" Alex bellowed, laughing meanly at my plight at the same time.

"YUUUUUUFFFFFFF!!!!" I blurted as I hit the, thank God, luke-warm water and all four of my so-called *buds* quickly pressed their hands on my back and fully dunked me, totally soaking me.

I angrily and hastily raised my head out of the water and shouted, "You stupid bastards!!! Look what you've done to me, GOD!!! This is a thousand dollar suit and my shoes are worth five hundred...you shit for brains guys, you've ruined... GLLUUUUBBBB..."

But before I could continue my swearing tirade, Ronald grabbed me from behind by the top of my head and under my chin and dunked me again under the jettisoning water.

"Yep, stressed out as can be, poor guy," Ronald laughed and a few seconds later hoisted my head back out of the water.

"FUCKERS!!" I snarled as Ronald maneuvered me into a position so I was now sort of sitting in the Jacuzzi and holding me tightly against him, his huge arms like a vise around my upper body. "You guys will pay for this suit...and for my shoes..."

"...and my attaché case as well..." I went on when I saw my attaché case floating nearby.

"Relax bud, your suit and shoes will be fine, it's just water after all," Alex laughed as he and Dennis reached under the water, grabbed my ankles and brought my feet up above the water's surface, holding them tight as Ronald still held me fast by my upper body.

"Bastards, get your mangy hands off me, all of you before I...MMMMMMMMMM!!!" I began but Ronald cut me off in mid-sentence as he, to my total shock and utter disbelief turned my soaked head toward his face and clamped his mouth down hard on mine.

I splashed my outstretched arms frantically against the water as the dumb muscle-head forced his tongue past my lips and into my mouth.

"RRRRRHHHHHH..." I roared as Ronald then swirled his tongue around and around in my mouth, the taste of beer and cigars assaulting my taste buds...and I also felt my shoelaces being untied at the same goddamned time.

"Oh yeah, kiss him the kiss of life," I heard Howard say as he sidled up next to Ronald on the other side of me. "It's a guy thing after all bud, *a real bromance*...HEH!!!!"

As he spoke teasingly and mockingly Howard was tugging at my beard.

BUT FUCK ALL THAT beard tugging and bromance crap, because I was being kissed by a dude and two other *dudes* were unlacing my wingtips and then I felt said shoes being yanked off my damned feet, SHIT!!!!

Once my shoes were off Ronald stopped kissing me, but still held me tight by the top of my head and under my chin, as Howard went on tugging at my soaked beard.

"You stupid assholes, what's the point of all this???" I reeled crazily, my head somehow spinning from the damned kiss I had just been dealt.

Then, to add insult to my soaked misery, Dennis and Alex handed Ronald and Howard my size eleven ruined wingtips.

"What in all hell…those are my shoes you mugs…" I blubbered crazily as next, Ronald and Howard filled my shoes with water and poured the water over my head. "HEYYYYY, stop this idiocy and foolishness now you guys!!! This has all gone far enough!!!"

"I think he needs more de-stressing," Howard said to Ronald as they each poured water over my head again and then tossed my shoes aside in the whirlpool Jacuzzi, along with my ruined attaché case, and not to mention the contents of my poor attaché case, important papers and documents from work.

"NO, NO," I ranted and Ronald, fucker that he is, dunked my head again under the water.

"GLLLUUUUUBBBB…"

This time when Ronald yanked my head back up I saw that Dennis and Alex were licking my goddamned feet, holding them by the ankles and heels and slithering their tongues up and down and up and down the bottom of my socks.

"H-HEY!!! Look at that shit, look at that, look at those mugs; they're licking my goddamned socks, what's up with that???" I babbled stupidly and at the same time not believing what in all fucking fucks I was seeing.

To shut me up Ronald turned my head so I was now facing Howard. Smiling leeringly Howard said, "Pucker up Greg," and proceeded to press his mouth against mine.

"MMMMMMM…" I crooned this time.

As Howard pressed his tongue against my lips I found that this time I did not resist the bromance kiss. The feeling of what Alex and Dennis were doing to my feet, the way they were licking and even gently and delicately kissing them, was amazing somehow. As the strange tingling sensations slithered up my calves and legs, I found myself slowly opening my mouth to Howard's kiss. And lo and fucking behold as well, my manhood was stiffening in my soaked suit trousers…*buds*.

"OH YEAH, oh yeah, that's it Greg, like they must say where you work, get with the program bud, get with the fucking program," Ronald said as he now tugged on my beard as Howard kissed and kissed me, his mouth also tasting of cigars and beer.

When Howard stopped kissing me, he and Ronald held me tight between themselves, rubbing their hands over my bearded cheeks, sliding their fingertips over my lips, making me kiss and lick their fingers, even going so far as to insert a few of their fingers at a time into my mouth and making me suck on them, and as they took turns tugging at my beard, something that I would find that they REALLY enjoyed doing. I watched fixedly as Alex and Dennis were now running their tongues up and down the sexy arches of my socks.

"Fucking fucks, what is this, *what in all hell is this?*" I asked no one in particular, my erect manhood raging now in my soaked trousers. "Supposedly straight dudes we all are, what is this shit...plunge and soak a guy, kiss him, tug his beard and lick his socks???"

"All that and much more bud," Ronald laughed. He kissed me a wet sloppy Bugs Bunny style smack on one bearded cheek, hoisted himself out of the whirlpool and sat propped on the edge, his big old feet dangling in the water, AND, his huge old cock sticking straight up, hard, rigid, and enormous.

Alex and Dennis stopped licking my feet, and then they, and Howard all took me by my upper arms and waded me in the water over to where Ronald was seated with his gigantic skyscraper of an erection looking up at the sky. I didn't need three guesses to know what was expected next of me, GOD!!!!

A few scant seconds later, with Alex, Dennis and Howard hunkered around me, I was half standing and half kneeling in the whirlpool Jacuzzi in front of Ronald, sucking his erection like my life depended on it, while Ronald himself sat there groaning in a guy's ecstasy and puffing on and smoking a freshly lit cigar... MY GOD, what was going on here???

"RRRRMMMMFFFFF..." I sputtered as I bobbed my mouth up and down and up and down on my neighbor's cock, him jackhammering and thrusting in my mouth like a madman.

"Oh yeah, oh yeah, that's it bud, that's it Greg, suck my cock, suck my goddamned baby maker," Ronald prattled, blowing mouthfuls of cigar smoke down at me.

From behind me my jacket was taken off, and then my tie, like my beard, was being tugged on. I didn't know who was doing what to me at that moment because my eyes were squeezed shut as I was doing my work...my work being to service Ronald's huge man-meat...JEEZ!!!!

"Yeah, oh fuck yeah, Greg really gets into this kinky wet shit," Ronald said as Howard next hoisted himself out of the whirlpool Jacuzzi and sat down on the edge next to Ronald, his feet also dangling in the water, his cock at full mast, not as big and gargantuan as Ronald's, but it would be a mouthful nonetheless.

And what a mouthful it was, as I next found myself chowing down almost hungrily on Howard's cock, Ronald sitting next to him and stroking himself while watching me.

Before I knew what had happened all four of my neighbors were seated on the outside edge of the Jacuzzi and I was being used like some cheap whore on a Saturday night, being made to wade back and forth in the water between the four men... ...and service each of their cocks for a few moments each. And to be honest, it seemed like I was only too happy to do it. Was this a bromance thing as well??? JEEZ!!!

To be a tad more playful, and maybe even a tad mean, Ronald, before I was about to suck his cock again, reached down, undid my soaked necktie and used it to blindfold me.

"There you go bud, like Olivia said in that movie, feel your way," Ronald laughed as he knotted my necktie behind my head.

I went back and forth in darkness, sucking my neighbor's cocks, licking their balls, and then, OH GOD, then, OH MY FUCKING GOD, one by one they shot their pent-up loads, right down my goddamned gullet. They forced me to swallow every goddamned drop of their good stuff...JEEZ...

When they were all sated and as I was then kneeling in the whirlpool catching my breath I heard the sounds of rapid movement all around me...and to my disbelief I was shooting my load in my suit pants...without even having touched my cock or having had it serviced, JEEZ, made to cum by four dudes who had soaked, kissed, beard tugged me and made me suck them off and swallow their manly juices.

A few moments later I reached up and with my hands shaking took the necktie turned blindfold from over my eyes. I quickly looked around and all four of my neighbors were gone...as were the ashtrays that had been filled with cigar stogies...as were the beer bottles and coolers...as were the clothes that had been piled up all over the place...AND...as I climbed out of the whirlpool I realized that my navy blue nylon dress socks were gone from my feet as well...

/The End/

Thinking of my good buddy on Facebook, Greg

TITLE: FOOT RUB
Author: Christopher Trevor

"Foot rub, a goddamned foot rub, of all things," Brian Smith, handsomer than handsome paralegal was saying to himself as he approached the day spa, which was located a few short blocks from the office building where he worked on Wall Street.

The fine-looking thirty-plus gentleman was smartly dressed in a dark blue suit, light blue shirt, a red silk necktie and lace-up well-shined black cap toe shoes.

"Of all things, *of all goddamned things* to relieve stress, my boss recommends a foot rub, and of all things even more goddamned, *my doctor* says that it's a *wonderful idea AND a wonderful form of therapy,*" Brian was thinking as he entered the spa. "Jeez, the way my size twelve dogs sweat all damned day in my silk dress socks and leather shoes I feel sorry for whoever the tech is that's going to be rubbing and massaging them. AH, fuck my silk dress socks and leather shoes, my feet stink even after I've been wearing my thick white or black sweat socks and sneakers while I work out at the gym, damn, stinky feet Brian I should be called. But the way I see it, it's the funeral for whoever gets elected to work on my stinkers at this spa."

As the door closed behind him Brian took in the most relaxing sights and scents of the spa's state of the art waiting room - the two plush soft mauve colored sofas faced each other across the room, and the aromatherapy machine set up on a regal looking end table seemed to be emanating a scent akin to jasmine, or perhaps lavender.

The walls were painted a color that looked to be what artists would refer to as Sahara Sand, and on another end table sat a vase of freshly cut well-scented red roses. Brian stepped across the sandblasted wood floor, the taps on his heels clicking as he went, and seconds later he stood at a chest level desk where a female receptionist sat. The nametag on her white blouse with the name of the spa emblazoned on one side read "Valerie." She had dark brown hair cut shoulder length, deep brown eyes and wore a minimum of make-up, although for the life of him Brian found himself somehow transfixed by the intense shade of her red lipstick.

Valerie looked up from the computer screen she had been working at and smiled.

"May I help you?" she asked, smiling.

"Uh yes, I uh, I have an appointment for a, for a foot rub, a foot massage, the uh, I signed up for the three hour session," Brian found himself stammering in reply.

"Yes Sir," Valerie said, almost crooning, clicking away at the mouse attached to her computer, scrolling through a list of names on the screen. "Are you Brian Smith and are you here for the de-stressor de-compressing foot therapy?"

Tugging nervously at his tie, Brian said, "Yes, yes that's me, and that's what I'm here for, the de-stressor de-compressing foot therapy."

"Okay, you've been assigned to Doctor Ivanta Teeklu," Valerie said. "She really is tops in her field."

"Uh, excuse me, doctor? A *doctor* is going to perform a foot rub on me?" Brian asked. "I thought this was the sort of place where people go for things like manicures, pedicures, body massages, that sort of thing."

"Oh it is, it is Mr. Smith," Valerie replied, gathering some paperwork as she spoke. "But you see we also keep several doctors on staff for clients such as yourself."

"Clients such as myself? What does that mean?" Brian asked.

"Well, according to what I see here," Valerie said, looking at her computer screen. "You're here for a therapeutic foot rub *and* foot massage, a stress relieving foot rub and foot massage, yes?"

"Yes, that would be right," Brian said. "My doctor said that my stress levels were too high so he recommended a foot rub."

"Perfectly understandable," Valerie replied, smiling even wider now, and suddenly Brian was able to detect the scent of her perfume, which mixed well with the scents emanating from the aromatherapy machine.

"So, with that in mind, we're not just a run of the mill day spa where people come for things such as you mentioned, manicures, pedicures, etc. We also offer therapeutic services here as well. You would be *amazed*, Mr. Smith, at how well our methods here of relieving stress are so much better than say, medication, psychotherapy, even meditation. AND, in your case your doctor was very astute in recommending foot rub and feet massage therapy, seeing as you have high stress levels. You would be astonished at how many of our nerve-endings are connected to our feet. People really are not aware of just how sensitive our feet can be and how they can also be a source of healing for us."

Brian grinned his killer grin that he knew always won the ladies over, squeezed his big hands into his suit pants pockets, rocked a bit on his heels and said, "I like the way you talk, *very* informative."

"Thank you," Valerie replied. "But I'm not just trying to sell you a bill of sales, I firmly believe in the therapy that Doctor Teeklu performs for her clients. AND, I'm guessing, based on the suit and tie that you work some sort of high-pressure cooker job, yes?"

"Oh yes," Brian said, still rocking on his heels and his hands still scrunched into his suit pants pockets. "I work nearby on Wall Street. It's a law firm, very demanding work, a lot of hours, very, very little time for a social life. As a matter of fact I haven't been out on a regular date in some time."

Valerie instantly saw where Brian was going with this and to change the subject she slid a small stack of papers across her desk to him.

"You'll need to fill these out before you see, Doctor Teeklu," Valerie said, affixing the papers to a clipboard. "You may have a seat over there."

"Sure thing," Brian said, reached into his inside suit jacket pocket and produced a gold Cross Pen.

As Brian took the papers and stepped over to one of the couches, Valerie asked, "Might you want some refreshment as well? We offer fruit juices of most flavors, smoothies..."

"A beer would be awesome," Brian chuckled as he sat down and crossed one leg over the other, resting the clipboard on his well-toned muscular calf.

"I'm sorry Mr. Smith, but we don't have any alcohol on the premises," Valerie replied.

"Ah well, can't blame a guy for trying, right?" Brian teased. "A pineapple orange juice would be awesome then."

"Coming right up," Valerie said; she picked up her phone and dialed a four-digit extension. "Hi, Ronald, could you please bring a pineapple orange juice to reception, and also let Doctor Teeklu know that her six o'clock client, Mr. Brian Smith, is here? Thanks."

She hung up the phone and looked over at Brian as he was filling out the necessary paperwork.

"Your juice will be here shortly Mr. Smith," Valerie said.

"Thanks and please call me Brian," he responded with a smile.

"Okay, Brian," Valerie said and returned to the work she was doing on her computer.

The receptionist had to admit that this young man *was* very handsome, very handsome indeed, she always had a weakness for men in suits and ties, but like most young men from the world of Wall Street he seemed to be very pompous and full of himself, or perhaps she was just reading him incorrectly. He had boyish good looks but was somehow mature at the same time. He had said he worked for a law firm and that was no easy career to manage. She hadn't noticed a wedding band on his ring finger…

As she typed away on her keyboard Valerie stole a glance over at Brian as he continued filling out the paperwork and a tiny devilish grin crossed her hot red lip-stick colored lips. She pressed an unseen button under her desk, and in the room where the orderly named Ronald was mixing Mark's pineapple orange juice a buzzer sounded.

Ronald smiled evilly and added a small packet of powder to the glass of juice, giggling fiendishly as he did so. It looked to Ronald like Doctor Teeklu had another special pigeon lined up for her coop.

The paperwork was pretty routine, Brian realized, your basic name, address, phone number sections, where the client was employed, how the client had come to be recommended to the facility, any health issues that should be brought to the doctor's attention before the therapy started, any diseases in his family bloodlines, etc. etc.

Brian wondered that if all he was here for was a goddamned three hour, a three hour foot rub foot massage (???) why he had to fill out paperwork based on his basic health. When he came across a question asking if he suffered from any sort of heart or breathing conditions, he laughed and proudly checked the box for "No."

Brian quickly sped through the rest of the paperwork, figuring that there was no need to really read it over, seeing as other than his stress levels, he had no real serious health issues.

A few minutes later a door behind Valerie's reception desk opened, and a very tall, easily over six feet tall if that, *very* muscular brown haired dark eyed gentleman stepped through it. He was dressed in orderly's whites and carrying a tall glass of pineapple orange juice. He politely greeted Valerie and made his way over to Brian.

"Mr. Smith?" the orderly asked as he stood over Brian.

"Yes, that's me," Brian said, looking up at the orderly and saw the name "Ronald Greene" on his nametag.

"Here is the juice you ordered Sir," Ronald said, setting the glass down on a coaster on the end table next to where Brian was seated. "I hope you enjoy it."

"Thank you, I appreciate that," Brian said and the orderly left the reception area the same way he had come.

Brian placed his gold pen atop the clipboard and picked up the glass. He took a long sip, realized how thirsty he had been and quickly gulped down some more, nearly emptying the glass in two swallows.

"Hmm, you really are stressed Mr. Smith," Valerie commented from her desk.

Smiling shamefacedly at her, Brian said, "Guilty as charged Ma'am."

After he had completed filling out the paperwork and had drank all the pineapple orange juice, Brian stood up and handed the clipboard back to Valerie.

"Thank you Mr. Smith, I mean, Brian. Doctor Teeklu will be with you shortly," Valerie said.

"Thank you," Brian replied as Valerie got to her feet and stepped through the door behind her desk, closing the door behind her, taking the paralegal's paperwork with her.

"Hee, hee, she is one hot looker," Brian said to himself and pumped a fisted hand in the air. "I can feel the stress melting away already."

The paralegal put his gold pen back in his inside suit jacket pocket and sat back down on the plush sofa, crossing one leg over his knee again and gripping his socked ankle as he now awaited the arrival of Doctor Teeklu.

As he sat there Brian glanced at his empty juice glass and for a fleeting moment felt a strange churning-like sensation in his loins.

"AHHHH," Brian muttered, leaned his head back and his manhood felt as if it were suddenly alive in his suit trousers. "MMMM..."

"Mr. Smith? Mr. Mark Smith?" Brian heard his name being called a short while later, although it sounded a little as if his name was being said as Meester Brian Smeeth.

He quickly opened his eyes, looked around the waiting room and realized where he was.

"OH, sorry, I must have dozed off," Brian said and found himself staring up at one of the most exotic looking Asian women he had ever seen.

"Ees no problem Meester Smeeth," the Asian woman said; she·was also dressed in medical office style whites, but a lot sexier than the whites that Mr. Ronald Greene had been wearing.

"Yeah, I've been under a lot of stress at work lately, and uh, that's what I'm here for, to relieve that stress," Brian said to the Asian woman, looking deeply into her very dark, seemingly captivating eyes as her silky black hair fell softly across the sides of her face and down to her neck.

"I am Makya," the woman said as Brian let go of his ankle and lowered his foot to the floor. "I am here to take you to Doctor Teeklu. She ees almost ready for you."

"Ah good, good," Brian said and climbed to his feet, straightening his tie a bit and smoothing out his suit jacket.

"Please to follow me, Meester Smeeth," Makya said.

"Yeah, sure thing," Brian said and as he followed Makya through the door behind the reception desk he could not help but take in the sight of her long shapely legs, the way her silk stockings seemed to accentuate her sexiness, and the way her definitely well-rounded small tight butt filled out her short orderly style white skirt.

Once again Brian felt a tingling in his loins, only this time the feeling was stronger than the one that had occurred earlier.

"JEEZ, what a time to be getting all worked up," the paralegal said to himself. "But she sure is HOT as hell. I wonder where Valerie went... They sure have hot looking staff members here..."

As these thoughts seemed to race through his mind Brian felt the churning in his loins growing stronger with each passing second.

"Even that guy who served me the juice was hot, in an erotic sort of way I suppose it can be said," Brian thought and then squeezed his eyes shut for a second and shook his head from side to side. "Oh fuck, what was I thinking just then???"

"The room you weel be in is down thees hall," Makya said as she led the way.

"Uh, cool, cool, say uh, what kind of name is Makya?" Brian asked, and the exotically beautiful woman halted, turned and faced the handsome suited gentleman.

"Eet is Japanese name, my whole name ees Makya Leekalot," Makya replied, then turned and walked on.

"Makya Leekalot???" Brian said to himself and had to stifle a laugh that was threatening to escape from him. "Leekalot??? Well, I can honestly say she could cause me to leak a lot, under the right circumstances of course, heh, heh, heh..."

They reached a room with the number two on it and Makya opened the door with a card key.

"Please to step een, Meester Smeeth," Makya said, and as Brian did, she closed the door behind them.

As he had done in the reception area, Brian looked around and took in his surroundings. This room was not as cheerful as the reception area had been; in fact it had a sort of medieval look about it. The walls were cold looking and solid red brick. Plain wooden shelves adorned the walls and Brian saw many, many massage supplies on those shelves, such as bottles of oils, lineaments, skin lotions, latex gloves, face pillows, scented candles, headrests and straps that looked adjustable. On another wall Brian saw hooks that were more than likely used to hang one's clothing.

The room was dominated in the center by a red leather massage chair that looked very comfortable, yet there was something sinister about it as well, and Brian quickly realized what it was.

The chair had what appeared to be stretched out wings on the back, and there were restraints at the ends of those wings. On the sides of the chair where one's wrists would be if the occupant's arms were dangling, there were also restraints. As Brian looked around he pursed his lips together and muttered, "Uh, nice, real nice," to Makya Leekalot.

"You are here only for feet massage, yes Meester Smeeth?" Makya asked Brian then, her stepping next the leather chair.

"Yes, yes, that would be it, Ms. Leekalot, a feet rub and feet massage," Brian replied, tugged at his tie and sat himself down in the red leather chair, stretching his legs up and onto the leg-rest, leaning himself back. "AH, nice, this is real comfortable."

"Glad you like Meester Smeeth," Makya said. "But you may call me Makya."

"Okay, Makya it is," Brian replied and then to his astonishment the exotic looking Japanese woman stepped to his elevated feet, lifted one in one hand by the heel and began unlacing his shoelace.

"UH, what are, what all are you doing Makya? Brian asked.

"Well, for feet rub and massage shoes must be off feet first Meester Smeeth," Makya explained, sounding as if she thought that Brian was as dumb as a stump.

"Yes, yes, that is true, but I can take my shoes off and..." Brian began, as Makya then yanked his left shoe off his sized twelve foot.

"No, no, eet ees part of my job to do thees for clients," Makya said as she dropped Brian's shoe to the floor and then he watched as she held his silk black socked foot in two hands, practically caressing it.

The musty manly scent of feet sweat and leather from his shoe did not seem to be bothering the Japanese woman in the least; if anything she seemed intoxicated by it somehow. In fact, as Brian watched her handling his foot, he again felt that churning in his loins. This time he really paid attention to the feeling that the sensation was causing. It was a feeling of sexual desire that was actually bordering on being primal... and Brian knew that he had never felt anything like it before. He fleetingly wondered what was causing it. And somehow, as Makya Leekalot handled his foot and as its scent filled the air, the handsome paralegal's loins tingled all the more. As he had done in the reception area he muttered a sound like "AHH" as the feeling in his manhood seemed to somehow envelop him.

"You have very nice feet, Meester Smeeth, they will work well for therapy that Doctor Teeklu does," Makya said happily; she set Brian's left foot down and went to work unlacing the laces on his right shoe.

"UM, yeah, glad to hear that," Brian replied, smiling sheepishly.

Why was watching this woman take his shoes off his feet for him getting him so worked up in the crotch, Brian wondered crazily? It was just his shoes after all... BUT...hadn't there been another time, another time not in the too distant past, when someone else had been at his feet and he had found himself becoming mysteriously aroused?

Although this time it seemed that he was more than aroused, this time it seemed that he was feeling a lust that was almost caveman-like.

It was when he had purchased the cap toe shoes he was currently wearing, and it had been a sales "guy" handling his socked feet that time, and for some strange and unexplainable reason he had found himself chubbing up in his suit trousers, as he called it when he became erect at the most inopportune moments.

After he had purchased the shoes he had not thought about the fact that he had become erect and all worked up in his suit trousers that day...but he was sure as all fuck thinking about it now.

Once both of his shoes were off his feet Makya asked the handsome paralegal to stand up for a moment or so.

"Uh, why do I have to stand up?" Brian asked. "I'm real comfortable here and..."

"Well, how else weel I get thee rest of your clothes off you Meester Smeeth?" Makya asked, again sounding as if she thought Brian was a dumb guy.

"HUH???" Brian blanched. "But, but I'm only here for a foot rub and foot massage."

"Yes, yes, but ees policy that client must deesrobe, no matter procedure he or she ees receeving," Makya said, sounding as if her job depended on Brian doing what she was telling him to do. "Your underpants and socks can remain on eef you weesh Meester Smeeth, but all else must be deesrobed."

"Are you sure that's standard, Ms. Leekalot, I mean, Makya?" Brian asked, again tugging nervously at his tie.

"Oh yes, yes, most standard as you say Meester Smeeth, please to not get me een trouble," Makya replied, almost sounding like she was pleading now.

"Okay, okay, no problem Makya," Brian said and stood up, a look of befuddlement etched on his handsome face.

"Thank you Meester Smeeth," Makya said, took the paralegal by his upper arm and stepped with him over to the hooks on the walls.

As Brian stood docile and with his arms at his sides, Makya helped him out of his suit jacket and quickly hung it on one of the hooks.

As the handsome executive was about to start undoing his necktie, Makya was instantly in front of him, and as she shooed his hands away she said, "I weel do that for you as well Meester Smeeth. Eet is my duty after all."

"Uh sure thing Makya, yeah, you can uh, you can strip me, yeah," Brian said softly, grinning almost stupidly now.

"Yes Meester Smeeth, streep you, as you say," Makya said, somehow sounding oh so damned sexy to Brian, causing him to take a VERY deep breath.

When his tie was undone Makya slid it almost seductively (if Brian didn't know better that is) off his shirt collar, draped it around her own neck and got to work unbuttoning his light blue shirt.

"Oh Jeez," Brian whispered, realizing that when Makya got to the task of helping him off with his suit pants that she would no doubt see the full erection that he was by then sporting in his briefs.

Being stripped by this beautiful exotic looking woman was definitely having that effect on Brian, along with whatever else had started causing the feeling earlier.

Once his light blue dress shirt was off him, courtesy of Makya Leekalot, Brian shucked off his white tee shirt, handed it to her and watched as she hung it all up on another of the hooks, but kept his tie draped around her neck. There was something about his tie dangling around the Japanese woman's neck that was unnervingly sexual for him, and was actually causing his erection to seep a bit in his briefs under his suit trousers.

As she stepped even closer to him it seemed to Brian that she was moving almost in slow motion, and at that point he *really* took in the fact that Makya Leekalot had the most luscious looking voluptuous breasts. My God, were her nipples actually pressing against the top part of her white uniform?? How sexy and sensual was that, the paralegal asked himself and gulped hard, his mouth filling with saliva, the desire to nurse on Makya Leekalot's luscious looking breasts overwhelming him. But the paralegal did all he could to remain focused and professional. He was in this place to relieve stress after all, not cause it to elevate even higher.

Then, as Makya reached for the clasp on his suit trousers Brian reached down and grabbed her hand, stopping her action, her fingernails though still on the clasp.

"UH, Makya, perhaps you should permit me to do this part," Brian said softly, practically whispering.

"But why Meester Smeeth?" Makya asked, sounding confused.

"Well, I'm a bit uh, how can I say this..." Brian began and Makya grinned from ear to ear.

"Please to relax Meester Smeeth, you are not the first that I have done thees part of my job weeth," Makya said and glanced down at the most paramount bulge that was tenting the handsome paralegal's suit trousers.

"Yeah, I sort of knew that, but uh..." Brian grunted breathlessly and looked down as Makya proceeded to do her work and undid the clasp on his suit trousers. "But I think that somehow...*with me*...that it's that you're, that with me you're somehow REALLY enjoying this end of your job...OH Jeez..."

"I enjoy all ends of my job, Meester Smeeth," Makya said and when she pulled the zipper of Brian's suit trousers down his trousers slid down his long muscular legs and pooled around his black silk socked ankles.

As Makya squatted down in front of him Brian took another deep breath and stepped out of his suit trousers so the Japanese woman could pick them up to hang on a hook. Looking down Brian saw Makya steal a glance...and a sniff, yes, she definitely sniffed, at his crotch area... ...at the bulge in his briefs, what he called the chub. The handsome executive though chose not to mention it.

As Makya got to her feet again, Brian now stood there in just his white briefs more chubbed up than he could ever have recalled being, and his black calf length silk dress socks. He watched as Makya hung up his suit trousers and then turned to him once more.

"You seem very nervous, Meester Smeeth," Makya said, hooking a slender hand around his now naked upper arm and stepping with him back to the large leather chair where he would have his feet rub and massage performed. "Deed I maybe do sometheeng wrong?"

"NO, no, you uh, you did everything right, *just right,*" Brian panted and clenched his teeth as his erection seeped pre seed into his briefs; he suddenly felt his testicles churning as well. "If I needed to be stripped then you did your job just great Makya, jeez..."

"I am steel not finished with you yet Meester Smeeth," Makya giggled and guided the paralegal back into the red leather chair. "Please now to put your arms at your sides ..."

"Huh? Oh yeah, yeah, sure thing, Makya," Brian said, panting a bit as he spoke and as Makya squatted down next to his left side on the chair.

Before Brian realized what had happened Makya had his wrist locked in the leather restraint that was on the left side of the chair.

"H-hey, what, what uh is this all about?" Brian asked, sounding a tad fearful at that point. "What are you, *what are you* tying me up for Makya?"

"But Meester Smeeth, I am not tying you up at all, I am preparing you for Doctor Teeklu, thees is all procedure, standard as you say earlier," Makya responded and dashed over to Brian's right side.

AND, before the paralegal could use his right hand to reach over and free his left, Makya grabbed it by the wrist and locked it in the restraint on the side of the chair.

"Hey, now wait just a minute here Makya, I signed up for a foot rub and massage," Brian prattled, wiggling his toes in his silk socks angrily as he spoke. "I don't recall agreeing to be restrained like this..."

"Eet ees standard, Meester Smeeth," Makya said with a stupid smile on her face.

"Alright, alright, enough with the standard stuff," Brian railed, clenched his fingers into big fists and yanked, pulled and wrenched against his bonds, to no avail. "JEEZ, I'm *really* all tied up here..."

"Doctor Teeklu will be with your shortly, Meester Smeeth," Makya said delightedly. "You are now all prepared for your therapy."

"Yeah, great, *just great* that she's going to reduce my stress levels, because I got to tell you, Makya, that thanks to this position you've put me in, my goddamned stress levels are now off the Richter scale," Brian ranted, continuing to struggle. When he looked up across the room, he saw Makya heading for the door of the room. "Hey, where are you going??? Don't leave me like this, all tied up in just my damned briefs and socks, JEEZ!!!!"

But then, Makya was gone and the door was closed behind her, her having even taken his tie with her that was still draped around her neck.

"Fuck, what kinds of craziness have I let myself in for here?" Brian asked out loud. He again wiggled his toes and felt another churning in his loins, this one even more powerful than the last ones. "JEEZ, what's come over me???"

The handsome paralegal then looked down at his crotch, saw the way his manhood was overly engorged, the way even his testicles made an impression in his briefs, made a sound of disbelief and leaned his head back...

He had been tricked, stripped of his executive armor, and obviously the recipient of a mickey. Just what sort of de-stressing therapy was Doctor Teeklu going to subject him to?

"ERRRRR!!!" Brian railed; he then bounced his feet up and down on the footrest and rattled his wrists in the restraints. "What goes on in this place???"

TITLE: FOOT RUB (CHAPTER TWO)

Author: Christopher Trevor

Brian estimated it had been nearly a half hour since Makya Leekalot had left him in the room, stripped to briefs and socks. A half hour of sitting stretched out in the massage chair and restrained at the wrists. Needless to say, Brian was feeling sexy and ultra-vulnerable as he sat there helpless. The churning in his loins was ridiculous at that point and the handsome paralegal had to wonder what it was about all of this that had him so worked up in that area.

"JEEZ, and totally fucking fuck at this point, what kind of crazy and mixed up place is this that I came to for goddamned stress-relieving therapy???" Brian asked himself. "Don't the fools who work here realize that stripping a poor guy down to his essentials and tying him up like this will only RAISE his stress levels?"

But as he continued to struggle in vain against the restraints, Brian found that he was now sweating a bit and that the erection he was sporting was even firmer than it had been a few minutes earlier. Actually, it was stiff to the point that it was almost painful. AND it felt as if his testicles were literally cooking up batch after batch of his manly juices inside them, JEEZ!!! He hated to admit it, but he needed to, HAD TO relieve himself orgasm-wise...but restrained to the infernal chair there certainly was no way *that that* was going to happen.

A few more minutes passed and then the door opened. Expecting to see Doctor Ivanta Teeklu, Brian instead saw the muscular orderly who had served him his pineapple orange juice earlier, Ronald Greene.

"Hello Mr. Smith," Ronald said jovially as he stepped into the room, wheeling a medium-sized cart ahead of him.

"Uh yeah, hi there, Ronald, say uh, where is Doctor Teeklu?" Brian responded in question. "I've been waiting quite a while here and..."

"She was unexpectedly delayed with another client, Mr. Smith," Ronald replied as he set up his cart next to Brian.

Brian saw that atop the cart there was a tall glass of the same drink he had had earlier, pineapple orange juice...AND... what appeared to be a most ominous device. The paralegal's face took on a quizzical look as he took in the sight of what appeared to be a set of stocks done up in red leather. As a matter of fact, based on the fact that there were also hooks set up on the sides of the stocks it looked like they were actually part of the chair he was seated in, or better yet, *literally* trapped in.

"So Doctor Teeklu sent you in to do my therapy Ronald?" Brian asked as Ronald picked up the set of stocks.

"No, not exactly Mr. Smith, only to sort of prep you for your therapy, and to offer you another juice, to make up for the time you've spent waiting," Ronald said. "Tell me, are you comfortable Sir?"

"Yeah, I suppose I am, but uh, this being restrained business has me a tad unnerved," Brian replied.

"Understandable, but it is standard, Mr. Smith, it is really for your own good," Ronald said and stepped with the stocks to the foot section of Brian's chair.

"So Makya Leekalot told me," Brian murmured. "Say uh, what all are those?"

"Oh these?" Ronald said as he stood with the stocks at Brian's feet. "These are part of your therapy, Mr. Smith. Makya should have hooked you up in them when she was here, but obviously she forgot. Now, if you don't mind, please lift your feet as high as possible so I can hook this device up to your chair."

"H-hooked me up?" Brian asked, and without thinking did as Ronald asked and lifted his socked feet as high as possible.

While the paralegal's feet were raised Ronald quickly hooked the stocks to the foot rest on the chair. Once that was done Ronald grabbed Brian's left foot and slid it into one of the holes in the stocks. Then, Ronald pulled a lever atop the stocks, and the hole seemed to tighten unforgivingly around Brian's foot.

"H-HEY...what are you up to here man??? My goddamned foot is stuck in that thing now *and* sticking out the other side..." Brian protested.

"Yes Mr. Smith, as I said..." Ronald began and next grabbed Brian's right foot at the ankle.

"Yeah, yeah, I know, it's standard, fucking standard, God damn it all man and CRAP, I'm being tied up even more here now," Brian railed as Ronald restrained his right foot. "JEEZ, I can't wait till this therapy is over. What a story I'll probably have to tell my buddies."

"That I will whole-heartedly agree with, Mr. Smith," Ronald said and gave Brian's right foot a tight, almost affectionate squeeze. "Now, how about another pineapple orange juice before your therapy starts?"

That said Ronald picked up the tall glass of juice and stepped next to Brian with it...

"Sure, uh, I suppose, but before I drink that could you tell me *exactly* what's in it?" Brian asked as Ronald positioned the rim of the glass at his lips.

"Of course Mr. Smith, it's as you requested, pineapple orange juice," Ronald said and tipped the glass a bit so that the contents were now being sluiced into Brian's mouth.

Brian gulped down the cold refreshing juice, not noticing how Ronald was grinning at him almost lecherously.

"MMM..." Brian crooned as the orderly seemed to be forcing him to scoff down every drop of the liquid.

When Brian was done drinking and the glass was empty Ronald said, "It also contains some very special nutrients and enhancers."

"*Nutrients and enhancers*?" Brian asked and arched his head back against the chair and took a deep resounding breath, because all of a sudden the churning in his loins had maximized to what felt like better than fifty percent of what it had been already. "OOOOHHHH man...WH-what the fuck did you make me drink, Ronald??? What are you doing to me here???"

"It's nothing harmful Mr. Smith, nothing like that goes on here at this spa," Ronald said, sounding as reassuring as possible. "It's all part of the stress-relieving therapy you came here for today, Sir."

"B-but I'm feeling real...well...really..." Brian stammered and squirmed in the chair, wiggling his toes crazily under his black silk socks.

"Feeling what Mr. Smith?" Ronald grinned devilishly now as he set the empty glass down on his cart and stepped over to Brian's feet.

"Well, just between us dudes, Ronald, I'm feeling real worked up in the crotch, if you get my meaning," Brian said, trying to laugh it off to no avail. "Actually, to be *real* honest here, I'm feeling like I could do three women in a row with no problem what-so-fucking-ever."

"AH yes Mr. Smith, I get your meaning, Sir," Ronald said and hooked both of his big hands around one of Brian's trapped feet. "Some of our other clients have said that as well, that after drinking a glass of juice with our nutrients and enhancers in it that they feel a bit worked up...*in the crotch*...as you so aptly stated. Some of the female clients who have drunk it have said that they become wetter than ever in their universe."

"Th-their universe?" Brian asked.

Ronald grinned, squeezed Brian's foot tighter yet, clenched his teeth and said, "Their pussies Mr. Smith, their *universe*, the thing that we men would go to war over. That very special place on women that we men can't get enough of, ah, the joys of a woman's universe, yes Mr. Smith? Would you agree?"

"Uh, yeah, but uh," Brian stammered yet again, watching with a look of total inquisitiveness on his face as Ronald REALLY squeezed his socked foot, massaging it a bit…and the paralegal had to admit it did feel rather good at that.

"B-but wouldn't it make sense to let the client know that he or she was drinking your nutrients and enhancers along with the juice you serve them?" Brian asked. "I mean, really Ronald…did you know it would have this effect on me? To say it plainly bud, I'm all chubbed up here."

"Perfectly understandable, Mr. Smith, but in one of the forms you filled out earlier you checked the column for yes where you were asked if you would be willing to consume any natural nutrients and enhancers we may offer along with your therapy," Ronald said and squeezed and kneaded Brian's foot harder and tighter.

"I did that huh?" Brian asked, wishing that he had read over the questionnaire more closely instead of rushing through it just to be done with it and to get on with his foot rub therapy. "Say uh, Ronald, is what you're doing there with my foot part of my therapy? Are you still prepping me for Doctor Ivanta Teeklu?"

"UM, no, not uh, not really Mr. Smith, I just realized that these are *really* nice silk socks you're wearing here," Ronald replied and then to Brian's shock and astonishment, the orderly pressed a fingertip against the bottom of his foot, pressed hard and began gliding that finger up and down and up and down in a very fast motion.

"WHOA!!!!! WHOOOOOOOOO!!!! HEYYYYY!!!! HA, HA, HA, HA, HA!!!!" Brian suddenly blurted and curled his trapped hands at his sides into big fists.

"OH SHIT, Ronald, that tickles, stop that, oh my God that tickles man, stop that right this in-ha, ha, ha, ha, ha, ha…this instant, oh shit man!!!!"

But instead, Ronald, as if he were suddenly hypnotized trailed his finger even faster up and down the meaty bottom of Brian's foot.

"YAHHHHHH, wh-what in all hell man???" Brian shrieked. "You-you're tickling my damned foot, HAR, HAR, HAR, HAR, HAR!!!!'

When Ronald began swirling his fingertip round and round the center of the bottom of Brian's foot, the paralegal found he was laughing harder yet, louder with each passing second.

"OH MY GOD, Ronald man, what, what all's gotten into you man???" Brian pleaded, laughing crazily.

"HEEEEE, HEEEEE, HEEEE, HEEEEE, please man, DON'TDON'TDON'TDON'TD ON'TDON'T oh for the love of mercy, DON'T TICKLE my feet man!!!! HARRRRRR!!!!!

NONONONONONONONO OH NO, my feet are so damned ticklish Ronald, HARHARHARHARHARHAR!!!!"

Brian arched his head back as Ronald seemed to ignore his pleas and went on and on tickling the tar out of him...

"WHEEEEEEE, what-what kind of crazy place is this that my danged doctor sent me to???" Brian squealed miserably and laughed uncontrollably.

After a good ten straight minutes of tickling Brian's foot and listening to the handsome guy laugh and plead, Ronald stopped and looked at the paralegal's other foot.

"Oh yes, very, very nice silk socks indeed," Ronald said softly as he hooked his big hands then around that foot, squeezing hard.

"Fuck man, my goddamned socks probably cost more than you make in a week, you tickle fiend," Brian railed through clenched teeth, his trapped hands clenched into big fists as he arched his head forward as well. "Now don't you dare tickle my other foot as well...OOOOOOOOOOO HEEEEEEEEEEEE!!!!!! HARHARHARHARHAR OH NONONONONONONONONONONONO RONALD PLEASE!!!!!"

Once more Brian found himself shrilling, screaming and laughing uncontrollably as the muscular orderly was once more tickling him. Brian felt the churning in his loins seeming to increase with each passing second as Ronald increased the tempo of what he was doing to the bottom of the paralegal's size twelves.

Ronald next held Brian's foot tight by the upper section, scrunching the paralegal's toes in his hand as he pressed the tips of his first two fingers against the bottom of Brian's foot, and trailed those fingers up and down and up and down and up and down and in a crisscross motion at what felt to Brian to be at least a thousand miles per hour.

"YARRRRRRRRRR!!!!! OH YOU BASTARD YOU EVILDOER!!!" Brian screamed. "HAHAHAHAHA, HAHAHAHAHA...Ronald, man, you don't...HAHAHAHAHAHA...you don't understand...I'm not a normal ticklish guy, PWAHHHHHHHHHH, I'm hyper tickle sensitive!!! HOLY SHIIIIIITTT, it's the way I was born, HARHARHARHAR, so please man, stop tickling my poor feet!!!!"

Instead of stopping though Ronald next squiggled all of his fingers on one hand over and over the center of Brian's silk socked foot in a circular motion.

"HARHARHARHARHARHARHARHAR, okay, okay, that's it you scoundrel, when Doctor Teeklu gets here I'm reporting you for this!!!! HARHARHARHARHAR, oh God, I can't stop laughing here, HARHARHARHARHARHARHAR!!!!!!"

"But Mr. Smith, *this is* part of your therapy," Ronald said snidely and squeezed Brian's toes tighter and tickled his foot harder yet.

"WHAAAAATTTTT???" Brian railed loudly through his laughter. "T-tickling my damned feet is part...HARHARHARHARHARHARHAR oh fuck, HARHAHRHAR, can't stop laughing here!!!!! T-tickling my feet is part...HARHARHARHARHAR, part of my therapy???"

"There, you finally got the words out, Mr. Smith," Ronald said tauntingly and went on scrabbling his fingers in a faster and faster motion against the bottom of Brian's foot.

"RHHHEEEEEEEEEEE!!!!!!" Brian screeched through clenched teeth. "I-I did not come here to be tickle tortured you bastard!!! HARHARHARHAR, HEE, HEE, HEE, HEE, HEEEEEE!!!!!!!!!!!!! Oh my God man!!!!"

"No? Where do you usually go to be tickle tortured Mr. Smith?" Ronald asked snidely and again returned to Brian's first foot, grabbed it at the toes section, the moistness and scent of the paralegal's silk socks not lost on him as he again tickled the bottom of that foot.

"V-very funny, *very funny indeed Ronald*," Brian cackled. "HAHAHAHAHAHA, oh God, when I start laughing my head off like this I can't stop, HAHAHAHAHAHA, it just gets worse and worse... HARHARHARHARHARHAR, Ronald, I'm begging you man, please stop tickling my feeeeeeeeeeeeeeeeet, YAHHHHHHHHHH!!!!!"

"But to seriously answer your question Mr. Smith, yes, tickling your feet is most definitely part of your therapy," Ronald said.

"B-but why??? WHY????? HEEHEEHEEEHEEHEEEEHEEEE, oh HEEEEEEE..." Brian pleaded. "How could tickling a hyper-ticklish-sensitive guy be part of his therapy??? HARHARHARHARHARHARHAR..."

"Well, it's to loosen you up nerve-wise, Mr. Smith. As Valerie told you upon your arrival, you would be amazed at how sensitive our feet are and how so many of our nerve endings are connected to our feet as well," Ronald explained.

"B-but...but you said that you weren't here to perform any therapy on me, HARHAR, HARHARHARHARHARHAR!!!!!" Brian sputtered.

"As I said, Mr. Smith, it was when I saw your silk socks that something in me just couldn't resist," Ronald said. "You're a rare gentleman when it comes to that aspect."

"PWAHHHHHHHHHH!!!!!!" Brian raspberried loudly, spittle flying from his mouth before he again erupted into loud and raucous peals of laughter. "HARHARHARHAR, HARHARHARHAR, wh-what in all fucks do my silk socks have to do with it all???

If anything Ronald, HARHARHARHARHAR, tickling my poor hyper-sensitive tootsies with my silk socks on them makes the feeling all the more intense than if they were bare, HAHAHAHAHAHAHAHAHA, OHHHHH GOD, OHHHH GOD, please stop Ronald!!!!"

"What I mean is, you should see some of the socks that some of the male clients are wearing when they come here for a foot rub therapy session," Ronald replied. "Socks that don't match, socks with holes in them, socks that are inappropriate fashion-wise, the list goes on and on. You Sir I can honestly say are a rare gem when it comes to that..."

"SO, so fucking glad I could accommodate your strange fetish!!! HARHARHARHAR, HARHARHARHARHARHAR!!!!" Brian reeled crazily. "HEEEHEEEHEEEHEEEHEE, HEEEEEEEEEEEEEEEEEEE, Ronald please... Y-you said yourself that you weren't here to perform my therapy on me...HEEHEEHEEEHEEHEEHEEHEEEHEEE!!!!"

"Did I say that Mr. Smith?" Ronald teased and then pressed his fingernail tips against the bottom of Brian's silk socked foot and trailed them up and down and up and down in a speedy manner.

"ARRRRRRHHHHHHH f-fingernail tickling me is worse you scoundrel," Brian hemmed loudly. "HEE, HEE, HEE, HEEEEEEEEE, HEEEEEE, HEEEEE, h-how long do you intend to tickle me for????

OH FOR THE LOVE OF GOD RONALD, HAR, HARHARHARHARHAR, I-I can't take it, I can't stand it man...HARHARHARHAR..."

Through his laughter tear-filled eyes Brian looked down at his raging erection in his briefs and saw to his utter humiliation that he was now leaking beyond unbelievably, as the front section of his briefs were soaked with his pre seed. His manhood and his engorged testicles made a most paramount imprint in his thin white cotton underpants.

"OOOOOOOOO GOD Ronald, being tickled also gets me so worked up in the crotch area, HARHARHARHARHARHARHARHAR!!!!" Brian blubbered through his laughter. "I'm so aroused right now it's crazy, HARHARHARHARHARHAR..."

"Good show Mr. Smith, then the therapy I'm performing before Dr. Teeklu gets to you is working," Ronald said. "Being aroused shows lower stress levels you see."

"B-but it's the fault of your damned potion that you tricked me into scoffing down that's part of the reason I'm hornier than a cat in heat!!" Brian disagreed.

Ronald chuckled himself, leaned down and to Brian's astonishment stole a quick kiss on the paralegal's socks and toes, stopped tickling him and said, "True that I suppose, Mr. Smith", and stood up straight in front of the still laughing executive.

"Y-YOU SEE??? YOU SEE MAN???" Brian demanded. "Even though you've stopped tickling me I can't stop, HARHARHARHARHARHARHAR, I cannot stop laughing!!!! Fucker you are, HARHARHAR, I CAN'T STOP LAUGHING!!!"

"I've only stopped for the moment, Mr. Smith," Ronald said and stepped over to where Brian's clothing had been hung up by Makya Leekalot.

"WH-WH-WHAT???" What do you mean you've only stopped temporarily?" Brian asked and then his eyes opened in total horror when he saw Ronald extract his gold Cross Pen from the inside pocket of his hanging suit jacket. "OH NO, NO, NO, you wouldn't, oh God, NO Ronald!!!!"

But Brian could only simply watch as Ronald quickly stepped back to his chair with his gold pen in hand, a look of total sadistic glee etched on his face.

"Ready for more, Mr. Smith?" Ronald asked, stepped in front of Brian's feet and pressed the tip of the pen against the right sided tootsie.

"RONALD, please, PLEASE MAN, as one guy to another, please do not tickle me with that pen tip...PWAHHHHHHHHHHHH HARHARHARHARHAR, oh you fucking guy, it seems, HARHARHARHARHARHARHARHAR, it would appear that my begging you not to tickle me only makes you tickle me all the more, HARHARHARHARHAR!!!!" Brian found himself shrilling seconds later as Ronald was trailing the tip of the pen up and down and up and down the bottom of his foot in another fast motion. "OH FOR FUCKS SAKE AT THIS POINT RONALD, HARHARHARHARHARHAR, I'm gonna die laughing in this damned chair!!!"

"I beg to differ, Mr. Smith, you're going to be a better man for it all in that chair when we get done with you here by tomorrow evening," Ronald chuckled.

"T-TOMORROW evening???" Brian shrieked, almost sounding like a woman at that point. "Buddy boy, I signed up for a three hour...HARHARHARHARHAR, HEE, HEE, HEEEEEEEEE...a three hour therapy session...there's no way I plan on being here till, HARHARHARHARHARHAR tomorrow evening!!!!"

As Brian ranted and raved, he bucked forward and backward uncontrollably in his chair/ prison. He clenched his teeth and laughed through them almost insanely as Ronald meanly increased the speed and tempo of tickling him with his pen's tip.

"That's where you're wrong Mr. Smith, because you see, I had Valerie change your session time in our computers," Ronald said mockingly. "So as of now you are scheduled to be here overnight, to get as little sleep as possible and to have as much therapy as possible, which will include the type of therapy I'm performing on you at this moment."

That said Ronald stopped pen-tip tickling Brian's right foot and switched to his left.

"OOOOOOOOHHHHHH OH YOU bastard, but, but that's, HARHARHARHARHARHAR, th-that's akin to having kidnapped me, FUCK, you've tickle-napped me man!!!!" Brian cried out, tears streaming down his handsome face now as he laughed, guffawed and even sounded almost like a hyena after a while.

"Not really, Mr. Smith, it's for your own good actually," Ronald interjected, held Brian's left foot once more by his now very sweaty toes and scribbled the pen tip round and round in a circular motion all over the bottom. "Someone with stress levels as high as yours needs all the foot rub therapy he can get."

"HA, HA, fuck you Ronald," Brian roared wildly. "Even though I'm the poor guy laughing his fool head off here, HARHARHARHARHARHARHARHAR, the joke is actually on you bud!!! HARHARHAHRHARHARHARHARHAR!!!!"

"And just how do you figure that Mr. Smith?" Ronald chuckled as he held tighter to Brian's toes, squeezing the tar out of them. Brian saw the orderly was sporting an erection in his whites.

Obviously tickle torturing a helpless guy floated Ronald's boat, Brian figured angrily.

"B-because I have a date tomorrow in the early evening, HARHARHARHARHAR, with a real pretty lady, HARHARHARHARHARHAR, GODDDDDD, I can't stop laughing again, HARHARHARHARHARHARHAR, I have a date, and if I don't show up I'm sure she will alert...HARHARHARHARHAR...the *authorities*!!!! She will alert the fucking *authorities, THE AUTHORITIES!!!!*" Brian stated emphatically.

"Now Mr. Smith, you'll be able to make your date, no need to go that route, it's just that I've taken the liberty of extending your therapy session a bit, and it will only cost you half of what we usually charge here," Ronald laughed and pen-tip tickled Brian's foot more and more and faster and faster.

"RHEEEEEEEEEEE, HEE, HEEEEE, HEEEEE, HEEEEE, fucking FUCKS, fucking totally fucks, I'm being tickle tortured to within an inch of my life, HARHARHAR, HARHARHARHARHAR, and I'm going to be billed for it as well, what a joke on me!!! HAR, HAR, HAR, HAR, HAR!!!!! Brian swore. "HEE, HEE, HEE, HEE, HEE, HEE, HEEEEEEEEE..."

For the next half hour Ronald alternated back and forth pen-tip tickling Brian's sheer socked feet, he massaged them a bit in between, and then resumed pen-tip tickling them again and again...

All the while the handsome trapped paralegal guffawed, cackled, screeched and literally hyena-laughed till he was sopped in sweat from head to socked toes...AND the pain-filled frustrated erection did not deflate once during the entire time.

"WE, we'll see what the partners in the law firm I work for, HARHARHARHARHAR, HARHARHAR, have to say about what you've done to me here tonight," Brian rasped when Ronald had stopped pen-tip tickling his feet after another fifteen minutes or so.

Brian sat there with his head hanging down in front of his sweaty chest, his most pronounced and very erect nipples tingling, gasping for breath, bouts of laughter still escaping him as he tried to speak normally. The room was scented with a mixture of the paralegal's manly sweat, including the scents emanating from his very tickled, very moist silk socked feet.

"You, you must know I work for lawyers, Ronald, they will hear of this," Brian managed to spout as the orderly returned his gold pen to his inside suit jacket pocket on the hook where it was hung. "And at this point I would think that Doctor Teeklu should have been in here. Where the hell is she while her patient is being tickle tortured??? I demand to see her, NOW!!"

Ronald stepped in front of Brian, gently squeezed each of his now very musty scented sweaty silk socked feet and said, "You make a good point Mr. Smith, I'll go and see what's delaying the doctor so profoundly at this point."

Watching as the orderly strode out of the room, closing the door behind him, Brian muttered to himself, "And not a minute too soon, *I will* know the reason why I was tickle tortured the way I was..."

As he reflected on what Ronald had done to him Brian's erection pounded away and throbbed with a life all its own, demanding release.

"OH GOD, I should have made him free my hands at least," Brian muttered, sounding almost sorrowful. "Hate to admit it in of all places like a doctor's office, but I really need a guy's sort of relief here...maybe even twice...GOD... Why was I born so damned ticklish and WHY does it connect so much to my manhood???"

A few minutes later the door to the room that Brian was in opened and a very tall, slender, long dark haired woman entered. She was wearing an emerald green dress that reached her knees, no stockings, and high heeled black pumps and over her dress was a white doctor's coat. She closed the door behind her and stepped up to face Brian.

"Are you Mister Brian Smith?" the woman asked.

"Yes, are you Doctor Ivanta Teeklu?" Mark asked.

The woman smiled and glanced down at her nametag and when Brian looked at the nametag his heart began pounding in his chest, once more at what felt like thousands of miles per hour...and he wasn't even being tickled...

...at least he was not being tickled at the moment, for as he looked at the woman's nametag he knew with certainty that *he would* be tickled yet again before he left this place of insanity.

"Yes, I am the doctor who is going to perform your stress-relieving foot rub and therapy Mr. Smith," the Japanese woman replied with no accent as she took a battery operated toothbrush out of a side pocket of her white coat. "But you obviously got my name incorrect. It is..."

But as the woman spoke Brian's sweat drenched lips quivered as he said, "In-indeed I did, Doctor Teek L U..." reading her name on her nametag the way it was "properly spelled out."

"OH MY GOD, oh my fucking God, your name is Ivanta Teek L U," Brian said, his eyes filling with tears of agony and woe. "Tickle you, your name is Tickle You..."

That said the woman grinned from ear to ear and clicked on her electric toothbrush.

"OH NONONONONONONONONONONONO, not there, not there!!!!"

Brian screeched as Doctor Teek L U pressed the speedily vibrating bristles against one of his jutted up nipples. "YEEEEEEEEEEEE, oh my God, my nipples are as tickle sensitive as my feet are Doctor!!!! PLEEEEEEEEASE..."

"That is a good thing Mr. Smith, so then therapy will work well," Doctor Teek L U said happily as she then pressed the vibrating bristles against the tip of poor Brian's other nipple and got him laughing even harder. "We have many, many hours ahead of us Mr. Smith; therapy will be good solution for you..."

After a half hour of toothbrush tickling Brian's nipples the doctor began massaging and tickling his feet next...and all Brian was able to do was laugh raucously and helplessly throughout the time of his "Stress-relieving therapy."

/Not The End.../

Thinking of Mark...

TITLE: OF FETISHES AND BUSINESS ATTIRE
Author: Christopher Trevor

For as long as I can remember I have always been intensely attracted to and captivated by handsome men wearing business attire. Dark colored suits, silk neckties, dark colored nylon dress socks (calf or OTC (over the calf) length), wingtip shoes, (lace-up or slip-on) cap-toe shoes, and occasionally loafers - all seem to drive me wild. When I was a teenager I used to ride my bike to the train station between five and six PM on weeknights just so I could see the handsome executives in their suits coming down the stairs after working all day at their office jobs in Manhattan. I loved how, in the warmer months, some of them would be carrying their suit jacket over one arm, their tie pulled down from their shirt collar and the first few buttons of their button down dress shirts undone, obviously showing how tired they were from a long stressful workday. I longed to be one of those men in suits and I longed to be with them, in every possible way. There truly is something very erotic and sexy about a handsome man all decked out in a business suit.

After I graduated high school I decided I wanted to work in an office in Manhattan. Because of circumstances in my life that for now will have to go untold I was not able to attend college, so it was directly from high school to working in Manhattan I went. Dressed in my own business suit I set out to various agencies in hopes of having them help me to find a job.

In those days, this being the early 1980s a person could just walk into the agencies right off the street, unlike today where you have to set up an appointment beforehand. This was also the days long before the internet. One of the first interviews I went on was when I was nineteen years old. An agency had sent me to the main branch of Chase Bank to interview for a job as a teller. (I would think that because of this interview that is where the character of Arthur Gimble was born for my stories "Licking Arthur's Feet" and "Tickling Arthur's Feet, seeing as I said in those stories that Mr. Gimble worked for "Chase Bank.")

When I walked into the office of the gentleman who was going to interview me, my breath caught in my throat. He greeted me very politely, his hand held out. I shook his hand and took the seat he offered me facing his desk. He was more than handsome. He had brown short cut hair, dark brown eyes, and very chiseled features. His face alone was driving me wild. His shoulders and arms looked extremely built and muscular under the crisp white dress shirt he was wearing. As a matter of fact it looked to me as though his arms and shoulders would rip the shirt if he stretched too much. (Through the years I have also found it to be very erotic somehow for a very muscular guy to be clad in business attire, crammed into that suit and those tight short dress socks.) As he began the interview he tugged on his silk necktie a few times. At this point looking back on it I don't know if tugging on his tie was a signal that he was trying to seduce me or that he just had a nervous habit of tugging his tie. I would have loved to reach across his desk and tug on that tie. When he leaned back in his chair and crossed a leg over his knee I thought my heart had stopped. He was wearing shiny black lace-up wingtips and black nylon ribbed dress socks. He continued tugging his tie with one hand while his other hand lay on his dress sock.

I never found out if he realized that I was looking hungrily at that foot on his knee, wondering how that socked foot smelled and tasted in that shoe. Anyway, I didn't get the job with Chase Bank but till this day I will never forget that handsome man who granted me my first job interview.

Riding on the trains to and from work I love having the luck to sit near or across from a handsome man dressed in a suit. Most times I try to discreetly check out their feet. I especially love it when the train is not too crowded and they can stretch those feet out in front of themselves. Therapists, psychologists and psychiatrists claim that you can tell a lot about a man from the kind of shoes he wears. I don't know about that except that certain shoes can make a man's feet look extremely sexy in a very erotic way. I have heard told that some men become cops, marines, soldiers and sailors because of the uniform and the erotic looking shoes and boots they get to wear with those uniforms. I sometimes wonder how many men realize how sexy they look when they roll those nylon dress socks onto their feet after having pulled on their white briefs or boxers. (I know of a woman who loves watching her husband get dressed in the morning. She says that he looks so vulnerable and sexy as he pulls those dark colored dress socks on.)

When men stand there wearing those knee length or calf length socks, their underpants, and dress shirt (while they button it up all the while still shaking off that groggy morning feeling after their shower) they look extremely erotic that it goes beyond any feeling that I can adequately describe. There is a certain vulnerability and sexiness about the look of a man wearing just his underpants, dress socks, and a crisp button down shirt. I love to watch a man get dressed for work in an office as much as I love watching that same man strip out of that business suit at the end of a long day. Or at the gym in the locker room I love watching how those business suited guys strip out of their work-day uniforms. Navy blue suits with pinstripes, charcoal gray, and dark brown, all drive me wild. As I have made mention to my good buddy Len, it makes me laugh inwardly how those suit guys quickly get their dress socks off in the locker room and cram them in their shoes before concealing them in their lockers.

I also notice how a lot of those suit guys will purposely take their shoes and socks off first, before taking off their trousers or suit jackets. It seems that lots of guys must feel very vulnerable about standing there in a locker room in their underpants and dress socks.

But, as on the train I try not to be too obvious about it in the locker room. However, one morning recently on my way to work I saw a guy sitting there in a gray business suit as the train pulled into the station. The seat across from him was vacant so I sat down directly across from him. He had to be more than six feet tall. He had the broadest shoulders and arms that I had ever seen, built almost like a football player he was. His skin was olive colored; he had silky jet black hair and beautiful features. I guessed his age to be either late thirties or early forties. As I sat there transfixed by his at least size eleven feet (he was wearing black cap toe shoes and black nylon ribbed socks) I saw him look over at me a few times. I thought for sure that he was straight and was angry that I was checking him out. When he moved his feet I saw that one of his socks was slightly fallen, revealing some skin of his leg.

Now *seeing that is enough to send me into a heated sexual frenzy.* (I don't know where these fetishes of mine come from but at this point in my life I have accepted them as part of who I am and I love the way they feel, the same way that a large percentage of straight men seem to have fetishes for women in red high heeled shoes.)

The following day the same guy was there again on the train when I got on. As I sat down across from him I saw him looking at me, sternly. I said "Good morning" to him with a slight smile on my face. He simply nodded and looked away from me. He was wearing a blue gray suit that day. Once again he stretched his feet out for my viewing pleasure. He was wearing dark blue nylon socks and black wingtip shoes. As I looked at those big feet of his my breath came in short gasps. When I looked up at him he was looking at me looking at his feet. Again he looked away from me. He got off the train at the stop before mine just like the day before and I was sitting there with my heart pounding.

The third day I saw him he was wearing a brown business suit. As I got on the train and was about to take my usual seat across from him he smiled at me and gestured to the vacant seat next to him. My heart thudded at what had to be sixty miles an hour. Slowly, as the train doors closed I walked over and sat down next to him. He crossed one leg over his knee, his foot resting on that knee. He was wearing brown lace-up cap toe shoes with brown nylon ribbed socks that morning with his suit. My eyes instantly locked on that foot just inches from me now rather than across from me. I could feel the big guy's eyes looking intently at me. It seemed at that moment we were the only two people on that train.

"How're you doin'?" he asked me with a real tough and macho Brooklyn accent.

"Fine," I replied, looking up and into his eyes.

He was looking at me intensely, that was for sure, sternly, and in a very sinister way. I felt like I was three inches tall sitting there next to him. I could not believe that I was actually sitting next to him. He smelled of some kind of after shave lotion mixed with soap. The tip of his shoe that was resting on his knee touched the side of my leg. I looked down at it and he placed a hand over his brown sock covered ankle. My breath caught in my throat.

73

"Look at me," he whispered sternly.

I looked back up at him, directly into his dark and sinister looking eyes.

"What's your name?" he asked me.

"Christopher," I replied nervously.

"I'm Kevin Sander," he said to me, not smiling.

"It's nice to meet you Kev-er, Mr. Sander," I said with the utmost respect.

"Is it?" he asked me.

"Yes Sir," I said to him, looking back down at his foot.

"Look at me," he said, clenching his teeth.

I did as he said. This was a man who was obviously used to being in complete control. I looked at him. He didn't soften for a second. He was totally dominant and in control of the situation that was unfolding. He looked around the train as it got more and more crowded as it went further along its route. Then he looked back at me.

"I've seen you checking out my damned feet, you pussy," he whispered angrily.

"Y-you have?" I asked him in reply, a bit taken aback at having just been called a pussy.

"Yeah, I have," he said, his foot still touching the side of my leg. "You got a thing for feet or something?"

"Yeah, but not just for any feet," I replied in a husky sounding whisper. "For yours I definitely do, especially for yours."

"Fucking guy's got thing for my feet," he said in disbelief, his eyes rolling in his head. "Fucking fucks, of all things."

I didn't look away from him this time...

"You'd like to touch 'em wouldn't you?" he asked me.

"More than that," I responded.

He looked away from me for a moment and I stole a look at his foot. My mouth was filled with saliva just looking at it. I could have drooled right there. I gulped hard and looked up as he turned back to me.

"Where do you work?" he asked me with a small smile.

"On Fourteenth Street and seventh avenue," I said. "You?"

"Rector Street," he replied. "What do you do?"

"I'm an inventory control supervisor for a jewelry company," I said. "You?"

"I'm the goddamned manager of credit and collections for a bank," he said. "Now tell me, what the fuck are we going to do about all this?"

"What do you mean?" I asked him, trying to play dumb.

He licked his lips and then smiled at me. I felt a little more relaxed at that moment. But then his smile vanished and that stern look was back in his eyes.

"What I mean is I know that you want to service my damned stinking feet," he said to me angrily. "And I'll admit that I love seeing a pussy boy service these size eleven and a halves of mine."

I looked down at his foot on his knee.

"Look at me," he said angrily.

"By five o'clock tonight my feet are going to be tired, foul fucking smelling and in need of some real attention and affection," he said to me sternly. "Think you can make 'em feel good for me?"

I gulped again and breathlessly said, "I would love to."

He smiled and held out his hand. I shook at it as he held my hand in a tight grip. Then, he let go of my hand and reached into his suit jacket pocket. He handed me a business card with his name and business address on it. He told me to meet him after work at five thirty PM in front of the office building he worked in.

"I live alone so we'll have plenty of privacy," he said to me.

"I can't wait," I said. "I'll be thinking of you all day."

"You'll wait," he said with a smirk. "I'm going to walk a lot more than usual on my lunch hour today. I want my feet and socks smelling real good and foul for you tonight. And while I'm walking I'll be thinking of you."

After a while we got to his stop. He looked at me as the train pulled into the station where he disembarked.

75

"Be there, five thirty," he said as he stood up and towered over me. "Don't chicken out pussy boy."

"I'll be there," I replied. "Have a nice day."

"Yeah, you too," he said with a smile and got off the train.

<u>That Evening</u>

The work-day didn't go fast enough for me.

All fucking day all I could think about was Mr. Kevin Sander's big executive feet. I pictured him at his desk, his feet stretched out under his desk, starting to sweat and stink in his shoes. I imagined him walking around the area where he worked on lunch hour, really pounding the pavement to get his feet and socks more sweaty for me.

I pictured myself licking and kissing his socked and then bare feet as he called me pussy boy. My manhood throbbed long and hard in my suit pants as I thought about the impending evening. But of course the work-day came to an end and I took a train downtown to the building that Kevin Sander worked in on Rector Street. When I arrived at the front entrance of the building he was just coming out the door. I walked over to him and said hello. He greeted me with a small smile. He towered over me. He held out his hand and I took it. His hand enveloped mine as he shook it.

"How was your day?" I asked him.

"Stressful," he replied and let go of my hand. "Yours?"

"About the same," I said.

"Are you hungry?" he asked me.

"A little," I replied. "But I can wait to have dinner later."

"I have your appetizers right here in my shoes," he said to me sternly.

I looked down at his shoes and saw that he was wiggling his toes in them.

"Look at me!!" he said sternly.

I looked up at him, right into those dark, sinister, and extremely sexy eyes of his.

"Yes Sir," I said, feeling a little nervous.

"Look at me pussy boy," he said; holding me there it seemed with those piercing eyes of his. "Fuckin' look at me when I tell you to...understand?"

"Yes Sir, I understand," I replied sheepishly.

We took the train to Brooklyn and arrived at his apartment about an hour later. In the bedroom he sat down on the queen sized bed and told me to remain standing. I did as I was told. He looked me over like I was merchandise in a store window.

"Take *your* shoes off, pussy boy," he said to me.

Again I did as I was told, leaning down to untie the laces of my wingtips and slipped them off my feet.

"Come here," he whispered, a fiendish smile on his face.

Slowly, I walked over to him and stood before him. With his big hands he undid my belt and unbuttoned my suit pants. They fell down around my ankles and I stepped out of them. He ran his thick fingers over my white briefs and snapped the elastic in them.

"Look at me," he said.

I looked down into his eyes as he looked up at me. For the first time I saw his expression soften.

"You're beautiful," he whispered and kissed my hard cock in my briefs, causing an electrifying shudder to course through me. "So fucking beautiful, pussy boy."

He looked at me for a few seconds more, his fingers toying with my briefs. Again he snapped the elastic in them and again kissed my hard cock through them, holding his thick lips to them a few seconds more this time. I shuddered and my cock throbbed harder than hard.

"Undress down to your briefs and then I'll let you undress me," he said.

At those words I quickly shucked off my suit jacket, undid my tie and pulled it off, unbuttoned my white dress shirt and took it off, and lastly I rolled my socks off my feet. My clothes were piled up on the floor as Mr. Kevin Sander stood in the middle of the room.

"Get the fuck over here and undress me down to my socks and under shorts," he said to me. "Fucking pussy boy, looking so hot in your damned briefs."

I walked over to him and helped him out of his suit jacket, hanging it neatly on a nearby chair-back. Next, he stood still as I slowly unknotted his silk necktie. The times I'd seen him on the train, how I had fantasized taking his tie off him, and now I was actually doing it. I noticed that his nipples were pressing hard and erect against his crisp white dress shirt. As I slid his tie off him I pressed my lips against one of his nipples under his shirt. He quickly grabbed a handful of my hair and meanly yanked my head back, away from his nipple.

"Owwww!!!" I cried out at the suddenness of his yanking me by the hair.

"Look at me!!" he said, still holding me by my hair, twisting it in his grip.

"OWWWWW!!!" I cried out, louder this time. "Y-yes Sir..."

"You came here for my feet, *I let you* come here for my *feet*, not my damned tits," he said, looking down into my eyes. "If, and I mean *if,* if you treat my stinking feet right maybe I'll let you worship my tits, and that's a big goddamned maybe, pussy boy!! Got it???"

"Yes Mr. Sander, I got it!!" I said in pain.

He let go of my hair.

"Finish undressing me, now!!" he commanded.

I unbuttoned his shirt, slowly revealing the large muscular and barrel-like chest underneath it. As I pulled his shirt off him his chest transfixed me.

"Oh my God," I whispered, looking at his chest. "Oh God Sir..."

His chest was totally rock hard and muscular. His pecs hung down real erotically and his nipples were the plump, silver dollar-sized.

"Like that chest of mine eh, pussy boy?" he asked me with a sneer. "Well, you know what you'll have to do to get a taste of it *and my tits...*"

To tease the fuck out of me he squeezed his big nipples. The fronts of them jutted out and the tips of them seemed to pulse with a life of their own. I could tell that Mr. Sander had very sensitive, very sexy nipples. I unbuckled his belt, unbuttoned his suit pants and they fell down around his ankles. He stepped out of them and then stood before me in just his white boxer briefs, brown knee length nylon ribbed socks, and his brown cap toe shoes. He looked incredibly sexy and vulnerable standing there in just his boxer briefs, shoes and dress socks, but trust me when I tell you that he was anything but vulnerable. The way his boxer briefs came down around his thighs and his socks rode up to his knees was incredibly erotic looking.

His cock was hard and enormous looking in the pouch section of his boxer briefs. It seemed to be throbbing in there and oozing pre cum like crazy. My breath came in short gasps as I stood there looking him over, taking in the sight of him, devouring him practically with my eyes.

"Like what you see eh, pussy boy?" he asked me.

"Yes Sir," I replied.

"Come on, it's time for you to service these smelly feet of mine," he said with total authority.

A few moments later Mr. Kevin Sander was stretched out on his bed with his shoed and socked feet dangling off the end of it. I was kneeling by his feet, awaiting his instructions. My position reminded me of my status where he and this whole scene were concerned.

"Okay pussy boy, you're going to do exactly as I tell you, right?" he asked me. "You're going to be okay with all this, right?"

"Yes Sir," I replied, my mouth practically drooling as I knelt by his feet.

"Kiss my shoes," he said to me, sitting up on his elbows. "And I mean kiss 'em all the fuck over."

I puckered my lips and did as he told me to do, kissing the sides, the tops, and bottoms of Mr. Kevin Sander's brown cap toes. I even sucked on the shoe laces a few times. When I was done, he told me to slowly, so fucking slowly unlace them and then slip them off his feet one at a time.

Again I did as he said.

"Ha, making you into a goddamned shoe salesman," he chuckled as I slowly unlaced his left shoe and slipped it off his foot, heel section first. "Fuck, all salesmen know to remove a guy's shoe heel first. How'd you know that pussy boy? Fuck, what a foot slave I got here."

I did the same thing in getting his right shoe off him as well...

Holding his left shoe in my hand I looked up at him...

"Okay, put that shoe to your nose and mouth and sniff the inside of it," he said to me.

I put the shoe over my nose and mouth and inhaled deeply. It smelled all musky and funky, shoe leather mixed with feet and nylon sock sweat.

"Deep breaths," Mr. Sander said, watching me intently.

"Yes Sir," I replied, my voice muffled by the shoe over my nose and mouth.

"How does that shoe of mine smell, pussy boy?" he asked me.

"Pretty raunchy Sir," I replied.

"Good, now lets see how you like the way it tastes, lick the inside of it," he said with a wicked grin on his face. "Lap up my foot stink that's in there. Then you can get to work on my other shoe."

I held his shoe a few inches away from my face, stuck out my tongue, and licked the inside of Mr. Sander's funky smelling shoe.

"Damn, pussy boy," he murmured and laid his head back down on the bed.

As I licked the inside of his shoe I looked even more hungrily at Mr. Sander's feet dangling off the end of his bed. That was what I really wanted and he knew it. He was going to make me wait as long as possible it seemed. I could not wait to get my mouth on those big feet of his. I worked feverishly licking and lapping the inside of his heated and raunchy smelling shoe, devouring his all day foot and sock stink. A few times I drooled in the shoe and sucked it up heartily. After a while he told me to stop licking his first shoe and to get busy with the other one.

I put his left shoe down on the floor and picked up the right sided one. The studly executive leaned back on his elbows, his muscles bulging in his big arms and watched as I sniffed the inside of his right shoe. Then, I licked the inside of it too. I could hardly wait anymore for him to tell me to get busy working on his feet. Fuck, I could already smell them; I was close enough to them after all. And if the scent in his shoes was any indication of how his socked feet would smell and taste I knew it was going to be pure ecstasy. My cock pounded long and hard in my briefs.

"Okay pussy boy now you're going to get what the fuck you've wanted since the first time you saw me on that goddamned train," he snarled at me. "Put that shoe down, *now!!*"

I did as he told me.

"Look at me!!" he demanded.

I looked up at him lying there all stretched out on the bed. He had the body of a damned football player. I wanted to feast on him everywhere. Every fucking part of him looked delicious, totally rugged and robust.

"You ready pussy boy?" he asked me.

"Oh Sir, yes Sir," I replied breathlessly.

"Look down at my feet," he instructed me.

I looked at his beautiful big feet and my breath came in even shorter gasps.

"Take one of my feet in one of your hands," he told me.

I wrapped my right hand around his right foot. It was so big and meaty that my fingers didn't touch each other around his socked foot.

"How does that foot feel?" he asked me.

"Meaty Sir," was the first thing that came into my mind. "Real hot and meaty…"

"Caress it," he said.

I ran my hand up and down his right foot, stroking it gently. I adored the way his nylon sock felt against his skin, so soft and moist, so sensual.

"Sniff that foot," he said to me.

I leaned forward and sniffed the bottom of his right foot. It smelled funkier and raunchier than the inside of his shoe.

"Lick it," he instructed me.

I stuck out my tongue and ran it up and down the bottom of his right foot, loving the taste of his smelly sock.

I could not believe it actually, all the times I had seen him on the train, all the time I had fantasized about him and now here I was licking and sniffing Mr. Kevin Sander's raunchy socked foot.

"Kiss it," he said with total authority.

I kissed the bottom, the sides, and toes of his right socked foot, licking it in between kisses, really sniffing at his stinky toes… Man, his toes really reeked through those nylon socks let me tell you bud.

"Yeah, you're a true foot slave pussy boy," Mr. Sander said to me, a wicked grin on his handsome face. "Suck my damned toes…"

Again I followed his orders, sucking his toes through his socks one at a time. I sucked them like they were cocks, loving the feel of them in my mouth. When he moved his left foot next to the right one I sucked both his big toes through his stinky brown nylon socks. I drooled saliva over his toes and sucked it up heartily, mixing the taste of my saliva with his foot sweat...Heaven. Mr. Sander watched with total satisfaction as I serviced his feet and toes.

"Okay pussy boy, kiss my socks all over, up and down," Mr. Sander said meanly.

I cradled his big feet in my hands by his ankles and began kissing his socks all over, working my way slowly up to his knees and back down again. I ran my tongue over the ribbed lines in his socks and then kissed them all over again, up and down, several times. I closed my eyes in ecstasy as I sniffed his smelly feet over and over again, holding them in my hands. He watched intently as I again sucked his toes. It was like I could not get enough of those feet, those toes, *his socks*...his very being was all over those socks and I just wanted to inhale all of him in. I could service Mr. Sanders' socked feet all night long if he told me to. But then, after about ten minutes of silence and watching me service his feet, toes and socks Mr. Sander told me to stop. I instantly did as I was told although I really didn't want to stop.

"Look at me," he said demandingly.

I looked up at him. He smiled at me.

"You're doing well so far," he said to me. "Now, roll those stinking socks off my feet and get busy licking my bare feet."

As I slowly rolled his socks off his feet Mr. Sander settled back on the bed on his back.

"Ahhhh now comes the real treat," he murmured contentedly.

I didn't know if he was referring to himself or me at that moment. When his socks were off his feet I pressed my nose against the bottom of his meaty right foot. It smelled more than foul to say the least. It smelled like he hadn't washed it in days. I licked the bottom of it, swirling my tongue all over it, sucking on it.

"Ohhhhh yeah," he moaned and squeezed his nipples. "Like I told you pussy boy, service those stinking feet of mine real good and maybe I'll give you a chance at these big tits of mine..."

I didn't reply. I was in ecstasy as I went on lapping at his big naked foot.

"Suck my stinking toes," he said to me.

I took the big toe of his right foot into my mouth and swirled my tongue all over it, licking it like it was a cock. I sucked on it like crazy, my head bobbing up and down.

"Ohhhhh fuck yeah," Mr. Sander moaned, his hand moving over the big throbbing bulge in his boxer briefs.

I took his big toe out of my mouth and slurped his next two toes into my mouth at the same time. I caressed Mr. Sander's ankles, calves, and legs as I sucked his toes. When I was done with the toes on the handsome executive's right foot I immediately got busy working on the toes of his left foot. He sat up on his elbows, looking down at me again.

"Fucking pussy boy doesn't need to be told what to do," he murmured happily. "Fuckin' great foot slave I got here... Fuck, but that feels good..."

I gently sucked his toes one at a time and two at a time also. When I had sucked all the toes of his left foot I ran my tongue over the tips of his toes and over the tops of his big feet. I planted small delicate kisses all over the areas of his feet that I had licked and licked them even more. When he moved his toes apart I didn't hesitate. I rammed my tongue between his toes and licked up all the sweat and smell between them.

"Ohhhhh fuck, ohhhh yeah you fucking pussy boy," Mr. Sander grunted breathlessly. "Love to have those sensitive areas between my cheesy toes worked on. Look at me, *now!!*"

I stopped what I was doing and looked up at him. He was looking at me intently, his breath coming in gasps. I could see that the bulge in his briefs was threatening to rip right through the cotton material.

"You're fucking driving me crazy," he grunted. "No one ever made me feel so fucking hot just from licking my damned feet!!"

I kissed one of his feet as a way of saying thank you. Then, I quickly looked back up at him.

"Fuckin' guy man, what I am I going to do with you?" he asked with a grin.

He saw my eyes move to his chest and settle on the big meaty nipples on that chest of his.

"Okay pussy boy," Mr. Sander said with a smile on his face. "Pick up my socks from the floor, roll those goddamned stinkers back onto my feet, and then you can have some tit. For whatever the fuck the reason it drives me nuts to have my smelly dress socks on while you're servicing me."

"Yes Sir!!" I said happily and picked up his brown nylon socks.

Quickly, I rolled his socks back onto his feet up to his knees and kissed his feet a few times each. Then, he sat up on the bed leaning over me, his big tits right by my face. With no hesitation whatsoever I ran the tip of my tongue over and over one of his nipples. He moaned and grunted contentedly and wrapped his strong legs around me as I knelt there in front of him. I ran my hands over his socked feet and calves as I hungrily slurped one of his big meaty tits into my mouth and went to work on it with total gusto. I sucked, nipped, kissed and bit Mr. Sander's tit. He cocked his head back in ecstasy as I caressed his legs and sucked one of his nipples.

"Fuckin' drivin' me more than crazy," he whispered.

I stopped working his nipple and looked up into his eyes. We stared into each other's eyes for almost half a minute, neither of us saying a word. Then, slowly I moved my head toward his crotch, toward that giant bulge.

He didn't order me to stop so when my face was just an inch or less from his briefs I stuck out my tongue. As I ran my tongue over the bulge, Mr. Sander placed his hand on the back of my neck. The bulge was indeed throbbing and it was hard as a fucking rock. I sniffed at the briefs a few times, loving the smell of them as much as I loved the smell of his socks. I buried my nose in the side of his briefs and inhaled deeply. It was all sweaty and musty scented.

"Oh yeah, you want my cock, don't you, pussy boy?" he asked me and squeezed the back of my neck.

"Y-yes Sir," I replied, looking up at him. "Yes Sir!"

I knelt back as he stood up, towering over me.

"Take my briefs off me boy," he said in a commanding tone of voice. "Slow..."

I reached up and hooked my fingers around the sides of his boxer briefs.

"Kiss them," he said to me.

I leaned forward and kissed his boxer briefs all over, especially on the bulge in them and on the outline of his two big balls in them. Oh God, his balls looked so hot in those briefs. I was trembling at that point. When I was done kissing his briefs I pulled them down a little on the sides.

"Slowly, pussy boy," he whispered. "You're not going to believe what you're about to see..."

I pulled his briefs down a little more, folding them down along the way. Then, when I got to the bulge in them and I saw the tip of his pre cum soaked cock, my breath caught in my throat. His cock was at least nine or more inches long, thick, fat and throbbing. As I slid his boxer briefs further down, revealing more of that succulent and giant man tool, my breath came in short gasps. Massive sized droplets of pre cum oozed out of his sexy piss hole and slid down the veiny shaft of his giant meat stick. I stuck out my tongue and sampled some of that pre cum. It tasted like Heaven. I pulled his briefs down till his balls were revealed. His sac was hanging low and I could see that his balls were just packed to the max with his man juice. He had two of the hairiest and sexiest looking nuts a guy had ever had.

"Look at me," he whispered.

Holding onto the sides of his rolled down boxer briefs I looked up at him, a pleading look in my eyes. I watched in tortured agony as he squeezed his tits hard. In response to his tits being squeezed his cock oozed more pre cum. Fuck, it was like his tits were the control knobs for his cock. I kept on looking at him. His cock was twitching and he slid it over my upturned chin, teasing me unmercifully. He smiled down at me, moved his hands behind himself, and grabbed his butt cheeks. His cock twitched some more. God almighty, he had the most sexually sensitive body in the world.

"Kiss my balls, pussy boy," he ordered.

I looked down, and still holding the sides of his briefs (it was as if I could not let go of them) I gently kissed his big throbbing balls a few times each. As I kissed his balls he squeezed his butt cheeks.

"Ohhhhhh yeah, feels fucking great," he sighed real throatily.

"Mr. Sander," I whispered. *"Please, Sir, your cock..."*

"Okay pussy boy, go for it then," he said. "Get those boxer briefs off me and suck my big meat."

I pulled the executive's briefs down to his feet and he stepped out of them. I leaned down, kissed his socks twice each and then moved back up toward his throbber.

"OH yeahhh," I crooned as I licked the sides of his pre cum soaked giant cock.

Then, I took his throbbing meat stick in my hand, faced it toward myself, and wrapped my lips snugly around the crown of it. Mr. Sander squeezed his butt cheeks hard and grunted breathlessly as I poked my tongue into his piss hole and swirled my tongue all over the crown of his cock. I began to slowly suck him. He leaned his head back and moaned in a man's heated passion as I sucked him a little faster.

"Ohhhhh yeah, pussy boy," he whispered breathlessly. "Fucking, pussy boy..."

I ran my hands over his socks, loving the feel of them against his feet, calves and legs as I sucked his cock harder and harder. His cock was so long and thick that I had to stretch my mouth around it till it hurt. His pre cum was sliding down my throat in what seemed like rivers. God only knew what kind of a gusher he would shoot when he came. I tugged on his big balls, holding them gently in my hand, squeezing them.

"Ohhhh yeah," he moaned loudly. "Getting fucking close now, pussy boy!!"

Mr. Sander rocked back and forth on his socked heels as his cock throbbed more and more in my mouth. Then, with a roar like a lion he came, pumping globs and globs of thick creamy jazz into my mouth.

"Ohhhhhh yeah, yeahhhh, fucking A pussy boy!!" he roared and grabbed the back of my neck.

His jazz filled my mouth and I gulped it down as fast as I could, still sucking that glorious cock of his.

What I could not manage to swallow slid out of the sides of my mouth and dripped down onto my chest. His jazz felt hot as it slid over my chest. I continued sucking the big guy, wanting to suck and siphon every possible drop out of his giant cock.

"Ohhhhh fuck, fuck," he panted breathlessly. "Fuckin' milkin' me..."

He pulled himself to his socked toes and gyrated his body seductively, his cock still in my mouth. Finally, when he was done I let his manhood slip slowly from my mouth. It hung there all juicy, slimy and semi hard, his sweaty balls looking real spent as they hung below his glorious cock.

"Look at me," he whispered.

I looked up at him and he smiled at me, warmly.

"Fuckin' hottest most beautiful fucking guy I ever met," he said to me.

This time I smiled fiendishly and quickly slurped that giant cock back into my mouth.

"Ohhhhh you fucker!!" he roared as I began sucking him again. "Damn sucking me right after I cummed and my cock is all slimy and sensitive feeling...fucking sadist pussy boy I got here..."

I managed to get Mr. Sander to shoot another delicious load for me, and before we finally had dinner that night, he made me service his socked and then bare feet all over again...

/The End/

Thinking of Mr. Blue...

TITLE: THE PADLOCKED HEARTS

Author: Christopher Trevor and Inspired by: Tommy from the Train

It was a morning like any other that Wednesday. I woke up, as usual at four AM, no need for an alarm clock. I'm totally synchronized when it comes to my job. I shucked the bed covers off and made my way to the bathroom, wearing just my white boxer briefs and black sweat socks from the previous day. Yeah, I'm a dude who sleeps in his underpants and socks, ha, ha, ha for me.

In the bathroom I flicked on the light and like any other morning, the first thing I did was shuck off my briefs, toss them into the hamper, stand there in just my socks and piss good and heartily into the bowl, grunting and groaning in relief. When I was done, I stood in front of the sink and looked at my groggy expression in the medicine cabinet mirror. I brushed my teeth, flossed and used two mouthfuls of Listerine. For me nothing beats a fresh tasting mouth first thing in the morning. I've heard other dudes don't brush their teeth till after they shower. For me there's no other way.

I reached down, got my socks off, tossed them into the hamper with the rest of the laundry, and turned on the hot water for the shower. I gave it a minute or so to really heat up and then stepped in and under the nice warm spray, loving the feeling as it undid the knots and tension in my well-toned and muscular body.

I exercise four times a week at a gym near where I live and my job with handyrepairman. com also helps to keep me in tiptop shape, when I'm assigned to jobs that test my muscles that is.

To be honest I love my job as a handyman. I get to travel all over the city of New York, I meet interesting people and unlike a lot of my buddies I'm not stuck in an office all day wearing a suit with a tie choking me. In my opinion a tie is a noose around a poor guy's neck, ha, ha, ha again.

I soaped up nice and thick and lathery with Irish Spring soap, used Clean and Clear to wash my beard and mustache, and then used Suave shampoo to wash and massage my bald head.

JEEZ, how my work buddies tease and razz me about my young twenty-five year old bald head. Every goddamned chance they get they're rubbing and even squeezing it, claiming it's good luck to rub a young dude's bald head. *Yeah, right*, lucky for them or maybe somehow lucky for me?

Once I was done showering I turned off the water, grabbed a towel that was hanging over the shower door and dried off, my manhood rock hard and sticking straight out, my big kiwi-sized testicles hanging low and sexy. Talk about a big bald head I laughed to myself as I looked down at my steely erection, all nine inches of it.

Grinning from ear to ear, my brown almond shaped eyes gleaming; I stepped out of the shower and padded naked back to my bedroom to get dressed for work. Yep, a day like any other...*so far.*

My uniform for the day consisted of another pair of white boxer briefs, a white tee shirt, white sweat socks, a pair of dark green workpants with a matching button down shirt, tucked in of course. Even though we work as handymen where I'm employed, we're still expected to make a professional appearance. We are representing the company, after all.

I finished dressing by pulling on a pair of giant black work boots that came up past my beefy calves. I rolled my workpants up and tucked them into the boot tops, completing my ensemble for the workday ahead.

Before leaving the house I flicked on the TV to an all-day news station to check the weather. I was glad to hear that it was going to be in the seventies and sunny, no need for a heavy-duty coat, just a light spring jacket would suffice.

I left the house, locking the door behind me, and with my big workbag clutched in one hand, headed for the subway station. I stopped at a twenty-four hour bagel store for a coffee and buttered bagel to scoff down while on the train, no time to stop and have a real leisurely breakfast, that's a pleasure reserved only for the weekends for me.

I arrived at the main office, the home base of my job. The owner had all the schedules ready and waiting for me and my handyman buddies. After the usual pleasantries, I was handed my roster for the day. I had three stops to do, all of them in midtown Manhattan. My last stop was around three PM and being that it would take me nearly till the end of the day, the owner told me that I could go straight home from there and bring in my paperwork in the morning. I thanked him, put my paperwork into my bag of supplies and headed out to the underground garage to get the company van that I would be using that day.

I reached my last stop fifteen minutes early, at two forty five in the afternoon. I hoped that the person I had to see, a Ms. Lisa Remington, wouldn't be too perturbed. A lot of these Manhattanites, as I have found out over time can be very particular when it comes to appointment times.

I was fortunate enough to score a parking spot directly across the street from Ms. Lisa Remington's luxury apartment building on Fifty Fourth Street. I quickly collected all the tools I would need for the job from the back of the van, stowed them in my big workbag and then called her number, using a company issued cell phone.

"Hello?" I heard a sweet sounding female voice on the other end.

"Good afternoon, is this Lisa Remington?" I asked.

"Yes, it is who's calling?" Lisa asked, suddenly sounding just a tad stern.

Ignoring the sudden stern tone of Lisa's voice, I went into professional mode and said, "Hello Ms. Remington, my name is Tommy. I'm from handymanrepair.com. We're scheduled to repair a baseboard in your apartment and I'm downstairs. I realize I'm a tad early and..."

"Ring bell number seven C, I'll buzz you in and you can come up," I heard Lisa say, cutting me off in mid-sentence as the phone went dead.

"Looks like this is going to be one of those days," I mused with a grin as I made my way into the lobby.

As in most Manhattan luxury apartments, the lobby was absolutely beautiful. It had mirrored walls and a decorative chandelier-like light hung from the ceiling. The floor under my boots was sandblasted wood.

"Nice, real nice," I said to myself, wondering how Ms. Remington afforded living in such swank surroundings.

"May I help you?" a man called out to me from the front desk – which I hadn't noticed until now.

A tall guy with dark hair and intense looking eyes stood behind the desk, which contained a console with an array of buttons with numbers on them. He wore a navy blue doorman's uniform and a nametag, which read "Richard", pinned to the left side of his jacket.

"Uh yes, I'm from handyrepairman.com, I have an appointment with Lisa Remington in apartment Seven C," I said politely to the doorman. "I already called her and she told me to ring bell number..."

As I spoke the doorman held up his palm, halting me in mid-sentence while he reached for the phone on his desk. He pressed a button; it was obvious he was waiting for Lisa Remington to answer.

"JEEZ," I said to myself. "Seems like everyone in this building has a better than thou attitude."

"Hello?" Lisa Remington's voice came from a speaker on the console, and from the doorman's expression he knew he'd fucked up by having the speaker on.

"Uh, good afternoon Ms. Remington, this is Richard down in the lobby," the doorman rambled, looking at the button he needed to turn off the speaker. "There's a gentleman down here from handyrep..."

"I already know he's here, he called me, he knows to come up," Lisa said impatiently, and then she hung up.

Richard and I looked at one another; I smiled apologetically, made my way over to the elevator, pressed up, and waited the half a minute or so for the elevator to arrive. I stepped in and pressed number seven.

I got off the elevator a minute or so later and walked down the hall to apartment Seven C. I knocked gently with two knuckles. It took a few moments but then the door was opened. Lisa stood there in a plaid red and black mid-thigh length skirt, black sheer stockings, high heeled back-less slip-on pumps and a low cut black silk top. Not what I considered the kind of attire a woman would be wearing while at home in the middle of the afternoon on a weekday, unless maybe she was going out after I was done.

"Good afternoon Ms. Remington," I said as she looked at me. "I'm Tommy from Handyrepai..."

"I know," she said, sweeping a hand through her long black shoulder length hair, interrupting me again. "Come on in."

She had a blank expression but her dark eyes seemed to be focused everywhere at the same time. I walked into the apartment and she strode behind me to lock the door. As I shucked off my jacket, Ms. Remington stepped in front of me, pointed to a nearby closet and sternly said, "Hang it up in there."

"Uh, yes Ms. Reming..." I began.

"It's Lisa," she said, interrupting me again.

After I hung up my jacket I stepped back to my supply bag. I squatted down over the bag and took out the paperwork that pertained to Ms. Remington's, er, Lisa's appointment, while she stood a few feet away.

"Okay, according to this, you need a baseboard repaired," I said, holding the paperwork and looking up at Lisa.

She nodded and said, "It's in the home office, you can follow me."

I quickly got to my feet and followed the lady into the living room. The apartment was well-lit from the sun due to the many windows. Judging from the furniture and general décor, Lisa Remington favored art deco, in other words, expensive. Works of art by Warhol, Haring and even Monet adorned the walls, making for quite a contrast.

When we reached the office Lisa pointed to a section of the wall near the floor where a big section of a thin wooden border had somehow come loose. It would have to be reset. The wall needed to be re-plastered as well.

"How long do you suppose it'll take you to finish with that...*Tommy*?" she asked me, saying my name almost dismissively.

"MMM, around an hour to an hour and a half tops," I said, looking at her from the side with my head slightly turned. "If I don't get it done today the company can always send me back or send someone else to finish it."

"That's satisfactory," Lisa said and turned to leave the room, leaving me to do my work.

"I'll do my best to get done as quickly as possible Ms. Reming...Lisa..." I said.

She turned around, faced me and said, "Why?"

"Well, uh, I'm guessing from the way you're so nicely dressed that you're going out and," I began, realizing that I may have just put my big booted foot in my mouth.

"I'm not going anywhere, but thank you for the compliment," Lisa said and a wave of relief swept over me. "Just do the work...Tommy..."

With that, she turned again and this time left the room...

I smiled a bit sarcastically and pushed down the "Fuck you" that I wanted to call out to her. I was there to do a job after all, but jeez, the way she said my name...

With my bag of tools and supplies in hand I stepped over to the damaged wall, placed my bag on the floor and hunkered down over it to take out the supplies I would need.

A few moments later, as I was using a flat trowel to shave away the excess plaster on the damaged wall, from behind me I heard Lisa say, "Can I get you some cold water, or an iced tea maybe?"

Squatting on my haunches, my rear pressed against my boots, I turned and smiled at Lisa.

"Thanks, Lisa, something cold to drink would be great," I replied and without another word she left the room. "Hmmm, not much for small talk is she?"

While Lisa went to get me a cold drink I resumed scraping the plaster off the wall.

I was really immersed in my work, when a short while later I heard Lisa returning, her high heels clicking loudly on the wood floor at her approach. I was mixing up some heavy-duty glue in a grungy bucket as Lisa came into the room.

"Here you are," she said, standing a few feet away from me by the desk where her computer was set up.

I looked up and watched her place a tall glass filled with what looked like iced tea and ice cubes atop the desk.

"Thank you," I said politely, noticing that Lisa now had a black silk scarf draped around her neck. If that was there before I hadn't noticed it.

She simply stared at me, and didn't say you're welcome, so I smiled and returned to my work, turning my back on her.

As I worked and sweated a bit I heard Lisa open and close a drawer somewhere behind me, probably on her desk. Then, instead of leaving the room, she paced slowly and methodically over to me.

As I was spattering the mixed glue along the wall, Lisa was suddenly standing directly over me. I found myself looking directly at her black back-less high heels. Being this close to me I was accosted by the intoxicating scent of her perfume. As I was about to look up at her she placed the tip of a thin leather riding crop against my lips.

"MMMM...what..." I began, but Lisa placed a finger over her lips and shook her head, "No", signaling that I was to remain quiet.

"Knees," she said softly. "Knees...Tommy...now!!"

My heart was thundering. What in all hell was going on here??? Did Lisa mean that I was to *kneel* before her???

"*Knees,*" Lisa repeated sternly.

Without thinking about it I put my spattering tool down and found myself doing as the lady had instructed.

When I was on my knees before her, Lisa slowly slid the black silk scarf from around her neck, stretched it out, and said to me, "Lean your head back...Tommy."

Trembling a bit, thinking she was going to use the scarf to choke me with, I did as I was told, and then she stepped even closer to me, so close that her crotch

93

was just about in my face. She leaned down over me and pressed the silk scarf over my eyes.

"Hey..." I began and I heard her say, "Shhhh..."

Once more, instead of trying to resist her or fight her off I did as Lisa said and then she knotted the silk scarf behind my head, blindfolding me, plunging me into total darkness.

The blindfold was scented a bit with Lisa's perfume...*and something else...*

When she was done tying the blindfold, Lisa asked me, "Are you afraid...Tommy?" and the way she said my name was again sort of mocking, but my God, my cock was trembling and stiffening up in my underpants under my work pants.

"I'm confused Lisa, what are you going to do to me?" I replied.

"I asked if you were afraid," she repeated.

"No, I don't think so," I said and then I found myself reaching forward in the darkness and running my hands over Lisa's high heeled back-less shoes, feeling them all around, loving the feel of the leather against her feet.

Then I was trailing my hands up her calves, loving the feel of her black silk stockings against them, loving the feeling totally...and being that I couldn't see somehow made it all the more intoxicating. I clenched my teeth and gripped the backs of Lisa's legs tight, *so tight*, and trailed my hands up and down and up and down, breathing heavily. The scent emanating from her universe between her legs, MY GOD, it was the same scent that was on the blindfold she had tied over my eyes. Obviously Lisa had had that silk scarf in her panties, pressed against her crotch no doubt, seeing as it was scented the way it was, MY GOD.

I heard Lisa take a deep breath and then she moved closer yet to me, meaning that her crotch, *her universe* was just about in my face now, and the scent was amazing, GOD, so fucking amazing.

I moved my hands up, up the backs of Lisa's legs some more, and oh my Lord, the feeling of the silk stockings against her legs, mesmerizing, enthralling and totally hypnotic somehow.

"Slowly, go slowly," Lisa ordered. "Tommy..."

"Yes, yes Lisa," I whispered and felt the tip of her riding crop against the top of my bald head.

I snickered a bit and began to say, "My fucking work buddies, they tease me and rub my bald he..." but Lisa slipped the front of the riding crop right into my mouth and said, "SHHHHH..."

Once more I did as she said. She teased my mouth a bit with the riding crop, making me suck on it, without even having told me to do so. Somehow I knew *exactly* what she wanted, but MY GOD, how I loved hearing her voice when she gave orders.

The next order Lisa gave me was, "Kiss it...Tommy", as she extracted the tip of the riding crop from my mouth and held it against my trembling lips. I did as she said and kissed the riding crop, all the while holding tight to the backs of her legs, not wanting to let go of them. I kissed the riding crop and was able to taste and smell my own breath and saliva on it. Then, once again Lisa ran the tip of the riding crop over my bald head, swirling it around up there, the feeling of that somehow causing my cock to get harder yet, FUCK!

What was this woman doing to me??? Never before had anyone done to me what she was doing. And even though I was blindfolded and couldn't see a fucking thing I allowed it to continue. How could I not??? Oh fuck, how could I say no to this??? If my work buddies could see me now, fuck that, if I could see anything now, ha, ha, ha for me again.

Then, as I held tighter to the backs of Lisa's legs, trailing my hands up and down them still, she pressed the tip of the riding crop against the back of my neck and trailed it along the skin back there. I grunted breathlessly as I always loved it when a girl would squeeze the back of my neck or kiss it, or lick it...or even trail a goddamned riding crop over it, MY GOD!!!

"Forward," Lisa said softly but breathlessly then as she pressed the tip of the riding crop hard now against the back of my neck, pushing my head forward...*forward*... toward her universe.

"Oh my God Lisa," I whimpered breathlessly as my nose and mouth pressed against her silk panties under her skirt. "OH my fucking God..."

"Lick..." Lisa crooned as she caressed the back of my neck with the riding crop and I felt her other hand then trailing over the top of my bald head.

I stuck out my tongue and began furiously licking the front section of Lisa's silk panties, sniffing heartily at the same time, gripping the backs of her silk stocking clad thighs now...

...and...AND as my hands trailed further upwards toward Lisa's ass cheeks I felt the silk and metal clips of the garters snapped onto the tops of her stockings.

OH MY FUCKS, I was living every dude's fantasy here...and on company time at that... ha, ha, ha for me, I would be getting paid for having a kinky experience.

"Oh my God Lisa," I whispered, having stopped licking her panties and wanting so badly to see the garters on her stockings, wanting to see if the panties I was licking were see-through, wanting to see Lisa's universe. "Please Lisa; take the blindfold off me...oh please..."

But my request was rewarded with Lisa reaching over and WHAPPING my rear with her riding crop, it making a scorching sound and my rear feeling the burn.

"UHHHHH..." I panted in the erotic pain.

"Lick!" Lisa demanded and I quickly did as she said and resumed licking her universe, through her silk panties.

A few times I dribbled liberally against her panties and sucked up my saliva, really, REALLY pressing my lips against her universe. I sniffed at it even harder...and I swear, my saliva had moistened her panties enough that I was able to feel her strands of universe hair through the silk material, *oh my God*...

With my teeth clenched, my hands now gripping Lisa's tight as steel butt cheeks and kneading them and with tears in my eyes under the blindfold I pressed the side of my face against Lisa's crotch...and consequently it smelled like heaven.

"Oh Lisa," I whispered and held tighter to her butt cheeks as she caressed the top of my head with her fingers and rubbed the tip of the riding crop against my rear.

"Lick..." she ordered and I quickly again did as she said.

This time though as I licked her universe through her panties I took a chance... I took a chance and let go of Lisa's rear end and with my fingers trembling and in blindfolded darkness I began peeling her panties down, sniffing what was underneath them at the same time, the sounds emanating from me almost of an animalistic nature.

"Yes Tommy, yes..." Lisa swooned a few seconds later when her panties were down to her ankles and I was again gripping her ass cheeks...and burying my tongue as deeply as possible into her universe.

At the same time my fingers were finding their way into Lisa's rear hole...

I felt her wiggling her body in front of me and oh man, did I want to see how that looked. Once more I foolishly requested, "Lisa, please, please, take the blindfold off me now...I've suffered enough..."

And once more I was rewarded for my request with a HARD whap on my rear, courtesy of Lisa and her riding crop.

WHAPPPPPPPPPP went the riding crop and I bellowed, "OWWWWW!!!!" and without having to be told this time quickly resumed licking and slurping and even sucking on Lisa's universe, teasing her sugar walls tongue-wise...and by then two of my fingers were diddling her rear end at the same time.

As I licked furiously at Lisa's universe she was by then having a difficult time staying balanced on her heels. I wanted to suggest that we should perhaps go into her bedroom but I didn't want to risk another stinging swat to my ass with that damned riding crop of hers.

I mean, okay, all I had to do was reach up and take off the damned blindfold, but my God, somehow I was loving every goddamned second of this trip that Lisa Remington had taken me on.

"OHHHHH, OH Tommy, Tommy," I then heard Lisa cooing as her riding crop dropped to the floor and she gripped the sides of my head now, kneading my earlobes as she began her orgasm. "OH YES, yes Tommy, yes Tommy..."

The way she was saying my name was like music to my ears, it sounded almost like she was crying. As she came and came like a banshee I meanly licked at her universe harder yet, prodding her rear hole harder yet as well, really forcing the woman out of her as she keened in ecstasy.

Even though I was blindfolded I knew Lisa was standing on her tiptoes as she orgasmed, her universe was drenched by then and I happily scoffed it down.

When Lisa was done cumming, she slowly caught her breath and let go of my face and ears. I extracted my fingers from her rear hole and leaned my blindfolded head down and panted breathlessly as well, grinning from ear to ear as I did so.

"AW man, aw my God," I stammered. "Lisa, I don't know what to say here..."

She reached down, gently took the blindfold off me and I looked up at her as she quickly pulled her panties up, not permitting me to see the universe I had just serviced and brought to orgasm.

Her top was a bit wrinkled, and I wondered if she had been squeezing and teasing her nipples through the silk material as she made me service her.

"Lisa..." I whispered as I looked up at her as she draped the kerchief/scarf that had been my blindfold back around her neck.

"Finish the work Tommy," she said, pointing at the wall.

"B-but, my time is up," I stammered as she turned to leave the room, looking at my watch. "I won't have time to finish...and not to mention I'm feeling all..."

"Then I guess you'll have to come back and finish another time, you did say that that was a possibility didn't you Tommy? That you could come back..." Lisa said and this time she did leave the room, stomping on her high heels as she went.

A look of disbelief came over my face and my cock raged in my pants...

I looked at the wall, at my unfinished work and knew that I would *have to* come back. I prayed that that would be the next day. I collected my tools and other gear and packed them into my big workbag. As I passed the desk where Lisa had placed the iced tea I took a quick sip of it.

As I was leaving Lisa's apartment she was standing by the door with a large brown envelope in her hand.

"I uh, I have to say Lisa that this was one hell of an experience, I hope my boss schedules me to be here to finish the job," I said as Lisa opened the door. As I walked out she handed me the large envelope.

I didn't open the envelope until I was in the company truck and when I did open it and when I saw what it contained I burst out laughing, as I held Lisa's panties in my hands. They were scented with her juices and my saliva...

As I started the truck I knew I would be returning to Lisa's apartment very soon...?

The End?

Thinking of Tommy

TITLE: STUCK IN AN EXECUTIVE ELEVATOR

Author: Christopher Trevor

If anyone had ever told me that what I am about to relate here happened to them, I would have said that they were beyond bonkers, I would have said that they were totally out of their goddamned minds. But if anyone had ever told me that something like this, *like this, GAWDS,* would have happened to me, well, I REALLY would have said that person was beyond bonkers. I would have said they had more than a couple of screws loose. But fuck, the fact remains *that it did* indeed happen to me...and right there in a stuck elevator at that, on one of the most crucial days of my life, the day of a job interview to work at a company that I had been pursuing since I had graduated college, just a few short months back.

My name is Dale Robinson. I'm twenty-three years old. I have very short brown hair with a somewhat receding hairline, an over brow people have told me that's pretty sexy as it makes my dark brown eyes look more intense. I weigh in at one hundred and seventy pounds. I keep in good shape by working out at a gym on a regular basis, three days a week of weight training with a trainer and three days a week of cardio, one day a week I relax with no exercise, Sunday being my day of rest.

I had graduated college in June and had been pursuing the prestigious mortgage firm of Cooper and Cooper and Stanley for the last two months or so by sending my résumé to their human resources director, Mr. Carl Dreyfuss, and also emailing the top managers of the firms with letters of introduction and all the reasons why I should be hired as part of their management team. It was in early August that I had received the first reply from their human resources director, Carl Dreyfuss, to tell me via a phone call that they were most interested in me. The phone call ended with Mr. Dreyfuss telling me that he would like to schedule an interview with me very soon. I was elated, totally overjoyed and jumping for joy after I had hung up.

The first interview I was granted was with one of the top vice presidents of the company, the senior Mr. Cooper himself. He was a distinguished gentleman of around sixty years old or so with silver grey hair. Throughout the intense and most nerve-wracking interview it was obvious that he was all business, no nonsense and totally executive in his practices. I made sure to let him know that I was his man, as I looked up to businessmen such as himself. It was in being that way that companies such as Cooper and Cooper and Stanley had survived the recent recession and remained viable and necessary. We ended the interview with a handshake and a possibility from Mr. Cooper that I might be called back for a second interview with their human resources director, Mr. Carl Dreyfuss...and I was also told that if I passed the second interview my future and career would be cemented with the firm. Needless to say I left there that hot August day practically floating in my wingtips.

It wasn't until early September that I got the call to come in for the most coveted second interview.

Thinking that Mr. Cooper had decided to pass me up I started looking into other companies, but then, the Tuesday after Labor Day, my phone in my small Manhattan apartment rang, and I was again floating on air when I heard Mr. Dreyfuss' voice telling me that a second interview, with him, had been requested by the senior Mr. Cooper and could I be there the next morning in the human resources department on the fiftieth floor at ten AM sharp? I of course said that I would be there, that I would be *glad* to be there.

I arrived at the hulking office building on Wall Street that housed the offices of Cooper and Cooper and Stanley and other top of the line companies. Dressed in a grey suit with a light grey button down shirt and striped silk grey and white tie, I walked with confidence in my black wingtips, clutching my attaché case tightly in hand. As I walked into the building lobby at nine forty AM, twenty minutes before my second scheduled interview, I convinced myself that this building would be my career home. Looking around the luxurious lobby I could easily imagine myself as being part of the family that inhabited this prestigious location.

I walked through the somewhat crowded lobby of other guys in suits and ties and ladies in their business attire toward the bank of elevators. I stood patiently in front of the elevators for one that would take me to the fiftieth floor and to my ultimate future, hopefully. When the elevator door opened many other people piled slowly in with me. Being that I was one of the first to enter, I found a spot in the back, stood politely and watched as mostly other men in their business attired piled in and pressed the button for their floor's destination, as I had done.

The elevator doors closed and being that it was an express elevator; it bypassed the first twenty floors. The feeling was one of slight lightheadedness as we sped upwards. I thought of the ascending elevator as akin to my career, heading upwards. But then, suddenly, the elevator seemed to jolt and then halted at what appeared by the lighted numbers on the just below ceiling panel between the thirty-third and thirty-fourth floors. A few of the guys, myself included, grunted in surprise while a fair amount of the guys all seemed only very perturbed.

"Oh jeez, not again," the gentleman standing next to me on my right stated irritably to no one in particular. He was dressed in a very expensive looking dark blue pinstriped suit and tie. "This is the third time in less than three weeks that this elevator has gotten stuck...and at the same place as well."

From the front section of the elevator another gentleman glanced back at the guy and said, "Wasn't the building management supposed to have an elevator repair dude here to fix this thing?"

"Yeah, they said they would have someone here very soon, I suppose very soon means in the next year or two," the gentleman next to me replied to the other guy, both of them sighing in exasperation.

"So uh, what do you mean? We're stuck here?" I asked the guy at my right, the guy at my left seeming to be busy with whatever work he had with him in a folder, not the least bit worried looking that we were now stuck in a crowded elevator.

"Yeah, but don't panic, they'll have us moving soon enough, the building management knows about this elevator, like I said, this is the third time in less than three weeks this has happened, and this is my second time lucky enough to be in here when it happened," the guy on my right said, smiling sarcastically at me as he spoke.

"Great, just great," I stated miserably. "I'm here for the interview of my life and I get stuck in an elevator, of all the blasted turns of events."

"Don't worry guy, everyone who works in this building knows the deal with this elevator, if you're late for your interview it'll be forgiven," the guy said, suddenly smiling almost lecherously at me, something that for the moment was lost on me, seeing as I had other more pressing matters on my mind.

"Uh, how long were you stuck last time you were in here?" I asked the guy. He was now grinning at me, and I could not believe what I felt next, as his hand that was closest to me seemed to suddenly be over my crotch area.

My eyes opened wide in total shock as he began an up and down rubbing motion on my crotch area and said, "Hmm, last time I was stuck in here for about a good twenty minutes or so, good thing its air conditioned huh?"

I looked at him incredulously as he continued massaging my crotch area, my cock suddenly rising to the occasion at his masterful (that's the only way I can describe it) touch. Without saying a word, looking at him in total shock as he now again faced forward I wondered what in all fucks he was up to. Jack me off in a crowded elevator??? Fuck, I and my college buddies used to play all sorts of pranks on each other, but this was unbelievable, man!!

I clenched my teeth and looked at him from the side and muttered a sound like "RRRR", not wanting to call attention to myself in a crowded and stuck elevator.

But he ignored me and then his fingers were grasping my suit pants zipper and slowly pulling it down, MY GAWWWWDDDD.

From the front section of the elevator two of the other suited gentlemen were talking about the last time they were stuck in this infernal elevator as well, sounding irritated as all hell. One said he had an important meeting to be at in less than ten minutes, glancing at his watch as he said it. In the middle of the elevator the chatter was the same, all the guys belly-aching about how the building's management had failed in their responsibilities to get the elevator properly repaired. But none of the guys in that elevator were suddenly being handled in a most inappropriate way, as I was. I reeled through my clenched teeth at the guy as he slid my suit pants zipper down, the whiteness of my underwear peeking through my fly.

"What in all hell Mister???" I whispered nearly insanely from the side of my mouth, my lips quivering and chills now searing through my being.

Jesus Christ on a bicycle but my cock was hard as steel at that point and my balls were swelling up with my manly juices as well. What in all fucks was this??? I was not a dude who got off on other dudes jacking him off in crowded elevators.

"HUHHHHH..." I huffed breathlessly as the guy then brazenly reached into my suit pants through the fly and his fingers worked expertly at extracting my hard cock AND my big juicy balls from the confines of my underpants.

Then, with no one the wiser, the guy next to me simply faced forward, as if he was just another businessman on the stuck elevator, and held my manhood in his huge paw of a hand.

Looking up at the panel of numbers he said, "Yep, stuck at the same spot as last time," and gave my erection a good hard squeeze, pushing back on it a bit at the same time, forcing me against the back elevator wall. I squeezed my eyes shut for a moment and listened as others in the elevator agreed with what he had just said.

Looking at him as he began (OH MY GOD) stroking my manhood I whispered in a womanly sounding tone, "Mister, please, what in all hell goes on here???"

But obviously he ignored me, and teased me by moving his huge hand (momentarily) off my now throbbing cock and down to my balls, cupping the tender and sweaty guys in his hand, fondling them almost lovingly...my eyes crossed.

Next, he retrieved my cock in his hand and as he held it tight teased the tip of it with the pad of his thumb, sending more chills through me and making me pre cum.

I did my best not to let the other dudes in the elevator know what I was being subjected to here, namely being wacked off by a stranger.

"Mister, please, let go of me..." I whispered in a begging tone. *"If you keep this up I'm liable to..."*

But, ignoring me again, he began stroking me once more.

"Oh my fucks..." I whispered, nearly crying now.

The guy standing in front of me, completely unaware of what was happening said to me said, "Relax dude, they'll have the elevator moving in no time," but did not turn to look at me as he said it. The guy with my manhood in hand then looked at me from the side, glee showing in his eyes and said, "Yeah, but does no time mean in time bud?"

I looked at him desperately and shook my head vigorously from side to side as he jacked me harder and harder and faster and faster, totally aware of what his snide comment meant...

Then, his timing was superb dudes, because just as I shot my load, seething breathlessly and as silently as possible, the elevator roared to life, masking my moans of passion as the guy caught all of my load in his big paw-like hand, and the elevator continued its ascent.

Once I was done creaming my load and the elevator stopped and opened at its first destination and a few dudes piled out, the guy let go of my cock, whispered, "You're welcome" and followed his floor-mates off the elevator as well, his hand smeared with my mess, JEEZ!! I quickly reached down, pushed my softened and spent cock back into my underpants and just as quickly zipped up my suit trousers. I breathed a sigh of relief mixed with disbelief over what had just transpired and then exited the elevator at the fiftieth floor. Clutching my attaché case I made my way to Mr. Dreyfuss' human resources office, following the directions of the receptionist I presented myself to.

I was asked to have a seat outside in the waiting area of the human resources department and that Mr. Dreyfuss would be with me shortly, as he was in another meeting at the moment on another floor. I thanked the receptionist and sat down in a plush comfortable chair in the waiting area, straightened my tie a bit and waited patiently, thanking God that the stuck elevator hadn't made me late after all...but still reeling and in shock over what had transpired in the elevator.

About ten minutes later I heard the receptionist saying, "Yes Mr. Dreyfuss your ten AM appointment, Mr. Dale Robinson is waiting for you outside your office." At the sound of Mr. Dreyfuss' approach I quickly got to my feet, smoothed out my lapels and when he turned the corner my jaw dropped...for Mr. Dreyfuss was the guy who had just jacked me off in the elevator.

"Holy fucking shit," I whispered as Mr. Dreyfuss grinned from ear to ear and approached me, his big hand held out to shake.

"Good to meet you Mr. Robinson, I'm Carl Dreyfuss," he said, and I hesitated before shaking his hand

He smiled again and whispered, "Relax, I washed my hand, after I was done licking it clean."

A look of total bewilderment came over my face but I dutifully followed him into his office as he led the way to where he would interview me...

I am thrilled to say I got the job and a great starting salary...and after Mr. Dreyfuss told me I had been hired, well, he insisted on jacking me off again...and he does every chance he gets...

/The End/

Thinking of Timmy Backman

TITLE: ANOTHER SPANKING GOOD TIME
Author: Christopher Trevor

It was a Saturday afternoon when Robert and I arrived at Master Jeff's apartment for what Robert thought was just an afternoon visit. Robert is a marine and he was home on leave for a week. When I had told Master Jeff that my buddy was taking a week leave from his base in Georgia, the spanking Master insisted I bring him by for some fun, and some endurance tests. Like any good marine Robert was clad that day in his dress uniform complete with black patent leather lace-up shoes and his white hat. He is six feet two inches tall, black and muscular. He looks a bit like Denzel Washington. What Robert did not know when we arrived at Master Jeff's apartment was that he was indeed in for a hard endurance test, namely a hard spanking and sexual work over at the hands of Master Jeff and myself. All marines love it when they're put through something like this by their best buddies, and Robert would prove to be no different.

"Well, here we are," I said. "This is the apartment."

Robert raised his fist to knock on the door but I quickly stopped him.

"Wait," I said. "I have to prepare you."

"Prepare me for what?" Robert asked curiously.

I took a long white cloth blindfold out of my pocket and held it up.

"Take off your hat, your jacket, and your shirt and tie," I said with an evil looking grin.

Robert looked at me quizzically and asked, "Now what in the hell would I do that for?"

"It's a surprise," I replied, producing a pair of steel handcuffs from my other pocket.

"Shit, you guys planned this, didn't you?" Robert asked him grinning now as well as he took off his hat.

Moments later Robert was standing next to me bare chested. I had put his clothes neatly in my gym bag. Just to mention here, the marine's body was beyond magnificent. It was totally fucking awesome. Robert's chest and shoulders were extremely muscular and pumped up, and his nipples pointed straight out like two small arrows, the size of silver dollars. His stomach was washboard flat.

"I feel kind of funny about this," Robert said as I tied the blindfold over his yes.

"Just relax," I said reassuringly. "You're going to have a lot of fun today."

Robert didn't resist as I locked his wrists behind him in the handcuffs and then looked him over. Man, he was *fucking smoking hot!!* And the white cloth blindfold against his exotically black skin made him look even hotter.

"Whoo shit," I said, grabbing the marine's muscular upper arms. "I almost hate to bring you in there to Master Jeff. "I'd really rather just keep you for myself."

That said I leaned forward and gave each of the marine's tits a fast suck.

"Hey man!!" Robert exclaimed. "What exactly is this all about? What in all hell have I let myself in for, huh, buddy?"

Again I told the over the top hot marine to relax and just enjoy it. I also told him that Master Jeff and I had worked hard to be sure that he had a great time. I let go of Robert and knocked on Master Jeff's door. Oh man, the fun was just starting.

Master Jeff opened the door and his eyes instantly lit up at the sight of the handcuffed, blindfolded and bare chested marine.

"Well hello there," Master Jeff said in greeting. "And just who do we have here?"

He squeezed Robert's nipples as I guided the marine into the apartment.

"Jeez, but you guys are really after my tits," Robert said.

"We're after more than your tits," Master Jeff said, closing and locking the door.

We stood on either side of Robert and we each caressed his big iron-like chest, his huge biceps, triceps and shoulders, and even brazenly licked his nipples. Robert was sporting a bulge in his uniform pants the size of a python.

"Damn, you guys are driving me batty!" the marine stated breathlessly.

"Let's get him out of those pants," Master Jeff ordered. "I want to get started on him."

Master Jeff held Robert balanced as I unlaced his marine issue black patent leather shoes and slipped them off his size eleven feet. I sniffed the inside of each shoe.

"How do they smell?" Master Jeff asked me teasingly.

"Like a marine, they smell like a marine," I said.

"Shit, is he sniffing my shoes?" Robert asked.

"Listen Marine," Master Jeff said, holding Robert's arm tighter. "You're blindfolded so you can't see what the hell is going on so don't ask dumb questions. *Got it?*"

"I-uh-got it," Robert replied as I slid his trousers down his well-toned muscular and oh so sexy legs.

I took the trousers off him leaving the hunky, black marine wearing just his white briefs and black knee length dress socks. What a fucking sight he was, let me tell you. Squatting in front of the marine I ran my hands over his tall socks, caressing his iron-like calves and shapely feet.

"Come on, let's get him shackled him up," Master Jeff ordered next. "I want to get started spanking him."

"S-spanking me?!?" Robert blurted. "SHIT!!!"

Moments later Master Jeff and I had Robert standing in an archway with wrist shackles attached to the sides of the walls.

"Look you guys, I really didn't come here for all this, ESPECIALLY not to be spanked!!" Robert said as Master Jeff caressed his hot ass cheeks.

Ignoring the marine's protestations Master Jeff ordered, "Let's get him shackled up! Take the handcuffs off him."

I released Robert's wrists and he made his move. He reached up, pulled off his blindfold, and tried to beat a hasty retreat as Master Jeff and I quickly grabbed him.

"You're not going anywhere, Marine boy," Master Jeff stated, holding one of Robert's upper arms super-tight.

The marine struggled like crazy in our grasps, all his training it seemed having flown out the window. Then, an idea struck me. I reached under Robert's briefs and jammed two fingers into his asshole.

"ULLLPPP!!!" Robert moaned at the suddenness of his oven being invaded in such a manner.

The marine stopped struggling as I fingered him, which gave Master Jeff the opportunity to shackle one of his wrists to the wall.

"Shit, shit, shit," Robert rasped.

"Ha, no marine can resist having his man pussy plundered," I chuckled and prodded my fingers deeper into Robert's oven, getting a few more good sounding moans of pleasure mixed with helplessness out of him.

Seconds or so later I had done the deed of shackling Robert's other wrist to the wall. I quickly tied the blindfold back over his eyes and made him lick my two fingers clean.

"That was a good idea," Master Jeff said.

"Yeah, and just look at that Empire State Building sized erection that's pre-seeding in his briefs," I laughed. "This hot marine loves this...so far.'

"I don't love any of this shit!" Robert loudly disagreed. "That's a-uh-a piss hard-on.'

Master Jeff picked up a leather paddle and gave the marine's briefs covered butt a hard whap with it.

"UFFFF!!!" Robert gasped. "Shit guys, what in all hell is this about???"

"I'm going to begin by spanking your hot and tight marine butt with your briefs on," Master Jeff said, giving Robert two more hard whaps with the leather paddle. "Then, the briefs will come off and you'll be paddled bare assed. How does that sound, Marine?"

"It sounds absolutely diabolical Sir," Robert responded miserably, but grinning slightly.

With that Master Jeff brought the paddle down three more times on Robert's butt, making the spanking total eight times so far. Robert had a way to go and a lot to endure.

"After I'm done paddling your butt with my leather paddle, I'm going to lay you across my knees and spank you with my hand," Master Jeff continued. "And then when I'm done, and if your attitude has changed, I may decide to let you go."

Master Jeff gave Robert's butt two more hard whaps with the paddle.

"UHHHH!!" Robert gasped. "That shit hurts!"

"You haven't felt anything yet!" Master Jeff replied harshly, giving the marine's butt two more whaps.

That was twelve so far. Then, Master Jeff really started whaling into the marine and I lost count of the whaps.

Robert squirmed helplessly in the archway, ranting in pain as Master Jeff paddled him relentlessly.

I squatted in front of the hunky marine again and licked his briefs in the front, massaging his cock through those briefs with my tongue.

"Oh God..." Robert whispered. "Pain and pleasure, pain and pleasure, what a twisted mishmash it is..."

The whaps on the marine's butt sounded like gun shots in the room and by then Robert was crying profusely.

"Some marine," Master Jeff said mockingly and continued the hot and cruel spanking.

I snapped the elastic in Robert's socks and continued licking his briefs, savoring the funky smell of sweat and pre-cum. Finally, after what must have been at least one hundred whaps Master Jeff stopped. Robert then noticed that I was playing with his black dress socks and licking his crotch.

"OOOHHH..." he moaned deeply as he caught his breath. "So that's how you're keeping yourself busy while this guy abuses the crap out of me.'

We all chuckled and then Master Jeff said, "Get those briefs off him now. He's in for a lot more!"

"Oh God no!!" Robert pleaded as I slid his sweat soaked briefs off him. "Please, please don't spank me anymore, oh *please!!*"

I wasn't sure if Robert was serious or if he was just playing his role, but his cock was hard as a rock, pointing straight up, pre-cumming, and huge, a real schlong if ever I saw one. The marine's balls were dangling low like two coconuts. I tossed his briefs aside and took his low-hanging nuts in my hand.

"Oh my fucking God, what a set," I whispered as I rolled the marine's testicles in my fingers, savoring their sweaty texture.

Then, Master Jeff brought the paddle down on Robert's bare ass. The spanking had resumed. I amused myself by licking and sucking on the marine's big balls and of course playing with his socks. Fuck, there's nothing hotter than a big hunky marine wearing a pair of thin black nylon dress socks, what a contrast, in my point of view that is.

"ARRRHHHH!!! And OOOO RAH you fuckers!!" Robert cried as Master Jeff spanked and whapped his ass harder and harder. "Please..."

By now the hunky marine was crying like a goddamned baby. Tears soaked his blindfold as Master Jeff paddled his bare butt harder and harder. By now Robert's balls were soaked with my saliva. I began licking the sides of his big hard cock. Pre-cum oozed real sexily from the marine's cock-slit as I crazily lapped at the sides of his throbber. That erection of steel told me that Robert was not exactly hating what Master Jeff and I were forcing him through.

"Oh God...he's going to suck me, I know it, that crazy buddy of mine is going to suck my goddamned marine sized cock," Robert whispered breathlessly.

And then, I could not resist anymore. I yanked Robert's balls down real low and gobbled his big fuck meat into my mouth.

"That's right," Master Jeff said as he continued the relentless spanking of the marine's butt. "Suck that cock of his, milk him good!"

"OOOOHHHH SEMPER FI!!!" Robert roared now in that mixture of pain and pleasure he had mentioned earlier.

I tugged his balls hard as I sucked his cock like a madman, swirling my tongue around it and poking the tip of it into his piss-hole. The marine's pre-cum tasted magnificent.

"OHHHHH you fucking guys!!" Robert panted.

Master Jeff paddled Robert's butt cheeks harder yet. A few minutes went by and then the marine announced that he was about to cum. I took his cock out of my mouth and grabbed it in my hand, holding it tight.

"OH yeah, I'm going to shoot a big load!!" Robert gasped. "Fucking guys are making me crazy here, going to cum like the marine I am."

And that's exactly what he did. He shot a marine sized load into my hand as Master Jeff went on and on paddling the fuck out of his butt.

"OHHHHHHH!!!!" Robert cried loudly.

The cum filled my hand and even dripped and oozed through my fingers. When the marine was done shooting his load Master Jeff finally stopped paddling him.

"You're a tough marine Robert," Master Jeff said, taking Robert's blindfold off for him.

"TH-thank you Sir," Robert said, catching his breath. "I do appreciate that."

I smeared the marine's cum all over his huge chest, massaging it gently onto his nipples. Robert moaned contentedly.

"Okay, let's un-shackle him and handcuff his wrists behind him again," Master Jeff ordered. "I want to get busy spanking his butt with my hand. I want you over my knee, Marine!"

"The only fucking place I'm going to be is the fuck out of here!" Robert stated as we un-shackled his wrists.

Again, when his hands were freed Robert made his move. He struggled like a true marine as Master Jeff and I grabbed his muscular arms tightly.

"No more spanking this marine you guys!!" Robert ranted miserably, struggling most valiantly, swinging his legs forward real sexily. "You tested my mettle and that is EEEnough I say...:

Once again I jammed two fingers into Robert's sweaty asshole.

"UHHHNNNNN!!!" he moaned.

The marine's rock hard body arched forward as I dug and dug my fingers deeper inside him. As he swooned in a state of forced ecstasy, Master Jeff did the deed of cuffing his wrists behind him.

"Dam it all you guys," Robert pouted.

I kept my fingers in the marine's hole as Master Jeff and I walked him over to the couch.

"If I had known that this was what you guys were up to when you invited me here, I would *never* have accepted the invitation!" Robert shouted. "Get your goddamned fingers out of my damned asshole!!"

"Oh yes you would have come here," I said teasingly. "Just look at your cock. You're hard again."

I finger fucked Robert as Master Jeff took a few sucks on his nipples.

"AHHHH!!!" Robert panted.

Moments later the marine was blindfolded again. Master Jeff sat down on the couch and I guided Robert across his lap, the studly marine's ass a ready target for the back of the spanker's hand.

"Damned fucker is going to spank me again!" Robert seethed through clenched teeth.

I sat down a few feet away from Master Jeff, lifted Robert's feet, and gobbled his sock covered toes into my mouth.

"You really like those big feet of his, don't you?" Master Jeff asked me.

"I sure as all fuck do," I said, licking and slurping at Robert's socked toes.

"Okay Marine boy, here's the deal," Master Jeff said, placing his hand on Robert's succulent looking ass. "Your cock is between my thighs. Your job is to cum as I spank you! Do you suppose you can manage that?"

To drive home his point Master Jeff gave Robert's ass a fast whap.

"I-I can try Sir!" Robert replied.

"The faster you cum the quicker the spanking will stop," Master Jeff stated.

At this point I wasn't even listening to Master Jeff because I was too busy licking and savoring the scent and taste of the marine's black socks. I held his feet up by the ankles and lovingly and feverishly licked them everywhere as Master Jeff began the hard spanking.

"YOWCCHHH!!" Robert yelped as Master Jeff's hand came down on his butt.

"Start jacking off, Marine boy!" Master Jeff ordered.

The marine rocked his god-like body up and down.

He was definitely jacking himself off between Master Jeff's thighs, and got a good rhythm going as I sucked and licked his socks.

Master Jeff spanked the marine's ass harder and harder with each blow and it wasn't long before Robert was ranting and crying like crazy. He rocked his marine-built body up and down, frantically trying to shoot his load.

"You know, Marine boy, I really hope that you don't cum for a long while," Master Jeff teased Robert. "I'm really enjoying this."

"ARRRGHHH!!!" Robert bellowed. "I'll cum soon, Sir! I can feel it getting close!!"

A few more minutes went by and then the marine grunted and shouted in a man's pain-filled passion that he was cumming. Master Jeff grabbed Robert's upper muscular arms and pulled him to a kneeling position on the couch. His cock freed from between Master Jeff's thighs, the marine was unable to shoot his load.

"OHHHHHHH...*please Sir,*" Robert gasped in utter frustration when he did not shoot his load.

Master Jeff held Robert meanly and tightly by his upper arms.

"You're really tormenting him," I said to Master Jeff.

"You didn't shoot that load, Marine boy," Master Jeff admonished and mocked Robert. "Looks to me like I'll just have to spank you some more!"

"OH NO!!" Robert screamed as his cock went semi-soft. "Please man, please Master Jeff Sir, my poor butt can't take it anymore!"

Master Jeff chuckled meanly and gave each of Robert's tits a suck before he laid him back down over his lap, the marine's cock again wedged tightly between his thighs.

"Okay Marine boy, going to shoot that load of spunk this time?" Master Jeff asked Robert.

"Yes, Sir, this time I will, Sir!" Robert replied with determination.

Master Jeff resumed spanking the marine's ass, HARD, and I again lifted Robert's big (and by then very erotically smelly) socked feet to my mouth.

"I can't believe that fucking guy is licking my goddamned socked feet!!" Robert shouted and Master Jeff spanked and spanked him. "YOWWWCHHHH!!!"

The marine rocked up and down as Master Jeff spanked him relentlessly yet again and I salivated madly over his feet.

Finally, Robert shot his load, crying, gasping, sweating, grunting, screaming and shaking, all in a kinky mixture of ecstasy and pain. Master Jeff finally stopped spanking the marine and we sat him between us on the couch. Master Jeff took Robert's blindfold off for him as I un-cuffed his wrists.

"You're okay big guy, a real good sport too," Master Jeff said, caressing Robert's chest and licking his nipples. "You did fine. You're a true marine to the core."

Robert cried like a baby as Master Jeff and I then sucked his nipples.

Later, after Robert was calmed down we were all sitting on the couch together. The marine was seated between Master Jeff and me. He was wearing his white briefs and black socks.

"I cannot believe this experience," Robert stated. "I mean, I cannot fucking believe that you spanked me, licked my socked feet, and I got off from all of it!"

"It just goes to show you what can happen if you let yourself go and let someone else take control for a change," Master Jeff said as he squeezed one of the marine's nipples, twisting it a bit at the same time, getting a good moan of pleasure out of Robert.

"Say, how about one of you guys getting spanked now?" Robert asked us, smiling, obviously thinking that he had just come up with a brilliant idea, ha.

"I don't know Master Jeff, what do you think?" I asked.

"I don't feel like being spanked," Master Jeff replied.

"Me either," I said.

From his sides I and Master Jeff looked at the hunky marine seated between us and before he could react we each grabbed one of his muscular arms.

"Looks like you're it again, Marine boy," Master Jeff said tauntingly.

"OH no, no!!" Robert gasped in disbelief as we yanked him meanly to his socked feet. "Not me again you guys! OH DAMN, my poor ass today..."

"Looks like it's going to be a long day Marine," Master Jeff said as we forced Robert back to the shackles on the wall.

/The End/

Thinking of Master Jeff

EPILOGUE: FROM CHRISTOPHER TREVOR HIMSELF, AND SOME OTHERS AS WELL...

Before I began putting the fictional stories together for this book, I asked various fellow authors, book reviewers, friends, and Masters, Rulers and submissives a host of questions that pertained to the subject matter for this publication.

As in the past, with other books I've compiled, the responses were varied, spot-on and opened the doors for very erotic and in-depth discussions, and the fact that the replies also inspired some ideas for new stories.

While the stories in this book are fiction, for some people out there the activities indulged in, in these tales are a way of life, OR a way of fantasy life.

BDSM, bondage, executive humiliation, cop abduction, tricked into being tickle tortured, spanking and being spanked, kidnap fantasies, uniform fetish, AND a host of other very provocative eroticisms are what filled these pages.

What makes these erotic activities all the more interesting and attention-grabbing is the fact that when the players indulge in the eroticisms they call play, it is consensual from both sides, both sides fulfilling a need for the other side.

The questions I put to some of my fellow authors, book reviewers, friends and Masters, Rulers and submissives are as follows:

What does the word "Subjugation" mean to you? My good friend, a book reviewer, replied by saying, "Subjugation, to me, means submitting with humiliation. I may be wrong about this, but I myself, being a tickle top have never felt the desire to be humiliated."

On another note an author buddy said that Subjugation means enslavement, or to be taken control of by force. In terms of S/M, it would mean the "power transfer" was taken, not given, and is total, both sides accepting their roles.

A long-time friend and advisor of mine, a total spanking Master, describes Subjugation as a "person who does my bidding without questioning me, knowingly taking off his clothes, standing in the corner or at military attention, and awaiting my instructions for how he will be spanked by me.

A good buddy of mine, who is a total Master and Ruler stated very well: "So, there are two anecdotal terms that might help out here...when I, as a Dominant and

Administrator of corporal discipline (and related activity) slowly remove my wide leather belt, I feel a sense of power over my present submissive. I may or may not use the belt on their bare butt; however, the sound of it sliding through the belt loops of my jeans is almost arousing in and of itself. My submissive admits as well that the sound of the belt being removed from my jeans usually brings shivers of anticipation AND some dread as well. So for me, that is what Subjugation means.

Also, Subjugation, to me, is the total submission, abasement and lowering of self that a good submissive will take on, if that is part of their relational dynamic with their Dominant. As I have seen though, not all submissives need Subjugation, as not all Dominants/Masters/Rulers require that level of commitment. I prefer some "spunkiness" and initiative in a submissive-just enough that they can function independently, but will report to me and *choose* to submit.

A spanking buddy of mine, a very sexy submissive young man had this to add: "Subjugation for me is the sexual excitement of being shamed and watched while being spanked, naked except for my socks and briefs and OTK (over the knee) of course, by men only.

A long-time female friend of mine said, "Subjugation means to me, a victory over a people, a conquest, the act of winning, NOT to be defeated.

A sinister styled author buddy of mine responded by saying, "Subjugation, to me means to be controlled or be made to be controlled."

My forever tickle hero and constant tickle victim from past books of mine said, "Subjugation is a powerfully and stimulating word for me. It means power, control, domination, and I can almost feel the loss of all of those in the presence of just the word "Subjugation."

On the heels of my tickle hero, it seems only appropriate to follow up with a quote from his nemesis, a total tickle Master, and he had this to say, "My idea of Subjugation is the act of dominating another individual (in my case, always a male), finding his weakness (usually and primarily his ticklish areas and then stimulating those areas) while causing erotic responses from him. I have found that focusing on what turns me on causes my willing and helpless male tickle-slave to become aroused and more and by what I focus on, even when it was never before considered an erotic focus for him.

And lastly, a new, handsome Asian buddy of mine said that for him, Subjugation means serving or being under the control of a Dominant or an aggressive Top, being totally dominated and at the will of another person.

Are you a Dominant, submissive, or do you perhaps relish the fantasies of both sides? My friend, the book reviewer responded to this question by saying, "One can be submissive as a Dominant or dominate as a submissive. There can always be varying degrees of either in any situation. Personally, I enjoy being on either side of this spectrum, given my mood at the time."

Strangely enough, my female friend said essentially the same thing, "This depends on whom I'm with and my mood at the time as well."

My author buddy who writes S/M fiction said, "As a writer of S/M I suppose I'm both, but personally, I'm a submissive.

The spanking Master I know stated, "I relish being the Dominant."

Once again my buddy, the total Master and Ruler replied most appropriately by saying, "I am totally Dominant and don't switch and I greatly enjoy watching my submissives strip down nude, present themselves to me for discipline, and proceed to take the position I require them to be in, to receive their chastisement."

My sinister author buddy said that he is a total Dominant as well, but added, "The thought of being controlled bothers me."

My sexy submissive buddy said, "I'm submissive (as you know) but can have a Dominant fantasy of spanking other men.

My forever tickle hero and victim replied by saying, "I suppose you can tell from the answer to your first question that I am a hopeless submissive.

I don't live a submissive lifestyle, but my submissive nature is directly below the surface and ready to come out and render control to a sexy Dominant."

My tickle hero's nemesis, the tickle Master stated," My role is always dominant! I have been in a situation in the past where another sexy guy bound me spread-eagle, and teased me sexually while prompting me with his ticklish feet near my hands and face, and the thought of getting the best of him got me over the hump and forced me to climax very intensely. I only met with him twice, and he did this to me the second time we got together as well. He is the only one I would consider my equal, and would allow to dominate me again in the future."

Lastly, my handsome Asian friend said, "I am a total submissive in every sense of the word and in play."

Are there any articles of clothing (or gear) that when worn cause you to feel all the more Dominant or submissive? The book reviewer said, "I don't believe so, being naked adds to the submissive's feeling for me. However, I will admit that being dressed in shorts while being Dominant over a naked submissive causes me to feel all the more in control."

My buddy the spanking Master said, "I want my submissives to be wearing nothing at all, OR, very tight jeans that emphasize the butt area. For me, it does not matter what I am or am not wearing, I can discipline either way."

My female friend responded with this: "I would wear an 'easy-to-take-off' black negligee. Although, being totally naked doesn't hurt either."

My sinister author buddy stated, "Not for me. When my subject is bound and helpless what I wear doesn't matter and I don't care if my submissive has a preference.

My handsome Asian buddy said, "I find that I feel all the more submissive when wearing a jock, torn underwear, or even a leather jock...and I feel all the more submissive if I am butt-plugged as well. It can be that I myself put the butt-plug inside me, or the Master or Ruler that I have submitted to put it in for me, either way, if I am butt-plugged it makes the scene all the more intense.

My spanking buddy had this to add: "Wearing frilly women's underwear and tops makes me feel all the more submissive for spanking and for other forms of sex as well.

My tickle hero responded with his two cents by saying: "OH MY GOD, just the reverse. The lack of underpants, namely my trademark kangaroo pouch undies, makes me feel much more submissive and dominated. My penis swinging free in my pants and subject to uncontrollable erections is a constant reminder of the fact that I am not in control. Although I do not have a current Master, either real or virtual (online) I have an imaginary Master that has me by the balls and is in control.

Lastly, when it comes to wearing any clothing that may be arousing for me, I have found that Christopher Trevor, the author of all my ticklish trials stories, seems to enjoy having me stripped down to my black office socks, and it doesn't matter if those black socks of mine are OTC (over the calf) or calf length, because I always wind up being tickled to near madness while stripped to them.

My tickle hero's loving tickle tormentor, the Tickle Master added, "My dominance is intensified when I wear skimpy underwear or jockstraps, and a tank-top (usually both are black.) This look makes me feel very powerful, and in control! I also feel more intensely domineering when I blindfold my ticklish slave."

If you are military or some sort of officer of the law (a cop perhaps) does the job give you a sexual rush, being that you are in a profession where you are in charge, or perhaps the wearing of the uniform? How do you feel when you put on your uniform? And on the other side of the coin of being in a profession where you are in full charge, what does the thought of being captured and used in erotic situations do to you? My book reviewer buddy replied by saying, "I do relish a fictional and erotic rape scene, mostly as the rapist, but if my partner wanted to act out with me being the victim, I would."

My author buddy had this to say where this question was concerned: "Police and military are authority figures and as such powerful images for a submissive that enjoys being forced. The few cops I've spoken to did not like to wear their uniforms for erotic play, though that may not be universal. I don't know about the military."

My female friend said, "Although this question does not really apply to me personally, I will say that when I see a man in a uniform it brings thoughts of powerful muscles and brawny strength."

The spanking Master also felt that this question was not applicable to him; however he did say that when he plays with what he calls "military brats", keeping them at a stance of military attention while naked tends to get him hot.

My buddy, the total Master and Ruler nonetheless felt that the question was most applicable to him and had this to say: "Speaking of uniforms and accoutrements, I have a long-time submissive who is a radar cop. When he reports to me for regular discipline and training sessions (and believe me LOTS of cops secretly want to be dominated!) and when he removes his uniform, he hands me his handcuffs and bends over a chair to receive his chastisement. He becomes very erect and stays that way as I position him and fasten the cuffs to keep his hands out of the way. He has told me how very humiliating it is for a cop to be locked in his own handcuffs. He loses the erection during his discipline, but regains it shortly after."

Like the spanking master and my female friend, my sinister author buddy also felt that this question was not applicable to him, but he had this to say anyway, "I know looking at a man in uniform is a turn-on for me, but only the thought of having him helpless and controlled by me is what rocks my erotic world."

My tickle hero was definitely intrigued with this question, seeing as this was his response: "I was in the military and an officer, one who is supposed to be in control, and in charge. The uniform made me feel so much more vulnerable to seduction and sexual domination; because I felt it put a target on my back. And I would love to experience a capture scenario and sexual interrogation, just as the captured ticklish character did in the book, "Timmy's Ticklish Trials.""

Why do you think certain executives in positions of power and total authority find themselves aroused in scenes of erotic humiliation? Once more, my buddy, the book reviewer responded first and said, "In my opinion it's a matter of stress relief. Many CEO's, company vice presidents, managers, etc. NEED the feeling of "Subjugation" in an erotic and sexual sense in order to relieve the never-ending stress of their powerful and pressure-cooker jobs."

My fellow author buddy had this to say: "Actually I knew a spanker who specialized in executives, especially older ones. He was also an ex-seminarian, which made that all the more interesting. As you know, I myself am into a number of "judicial"

119

scenes-arrest, jail, and the like. It's not an uncommon fantasy that a cop or prison guard (whose jobs can be pressure-cooker stressful, just like an executive) gets his comeuppance from a con or a suspect (or a group of them.) Of course, that might lead to more problems for the con or suspect. While on the other hand, the politics of the humiliated executive might amuse some Marxists I know, seeing as it's a powerful fantasy on both sides. It's not just being stripped of power (if not a power suit), but also becoming a "second-class citizen." For a feeling of complete loss of power there is nothing like someone in a police uniform snapping a pair of handcuffs around your wrists."

The spanking Master simply said, "They are in need and needy of giving up some or all of their power."

Very notably, my sinister author buddy said, "Purely speculative on my part, but I've always thought that executives spend most of their days being responsible for decisions and once in a while they love to be freed (in a sexual sense) and let someone else make the decisions for them, even if that means being told what to do or even made to perform acts of utter humiliation."

My female friend added, "For certain executives, it may represent a stereotype of a person we learn to know, that shows a humbling to that humiliation and feel we can surrender our desires to someone else who can fulfill them for us, VERY SEXY!"

My handsome Asian buddy, the total submissive, added this: "Executives are in control and in power. Additionally, they hold others accountable and in some instances create fear in others, so when they submit they essentially give up that control and it is in a way a release and maybe alleviates the guilt they may be feeling of having caused other people fear and mental pain."

My spanking buddy had this to say where executives are concerned: "Certain executives who wield power get off very strongly on being submissive, as the change of roles allows them to decompress their emotions and explore a sexual side that they find difficult to admit to in the real world."

My tickle hero, an executive himself in the real world, had this to say about executives and erotic scenes of humiliation: "First, I think executives in positions of power have a latent submissive streak. It's there whether or not they know or admit to it. And scenes of erotic humiliation cause that submissiveness to surface. Also, leadership can be lonely and giving up control is a way to extract one's self from that position."

Finally, the tickle Master said, "My experience helps me understand the high-powered executives who have a weakness (especially ticklishness), and are in control of the financial or legal destiny of others relish in giving over control while being in an intimate situation.

The responsibility of making decisions and being in control offers no relief; therefore, they are most satisfied when that power is given over to one they trust, and one who knows how to release all the pressure that builds up. I've been fortunate enough to meet up with two such individuals, and they were SOOOO much fun to play with!"

So with all this in mind, I have given you, my constant and some new readers well, Christopher Trevor's collection of stories of: Rulers and Submissives of Subjugation." I do hope you enjoyed this book and I am looking forward to creating the next one, which will contain sequels for all of these stories. You may email me at ExecSocks@aol.com

Printed in the United States
By Bookmasters